Jessie Fremont O'Donnell

Love Poems of Three Centuries, from 1590 to 1890

Second Series

Jessie Fremont O'Donnell

Love Poems of Three Centuries, from 1590 to 1890
Second Series

ISBN/EAN: 9783337407063

Printed in Europe, USA, Canada, Australia, Japan

Cover: Foto ©Andreas Hilbeck / pixelio.de

More available books at **www.hansebooks.com**

LOVE POEMS OF : : THREE CENTURIES : 1590–1890 : : : : : :

COMPILED BY

JESSIE F. O'DONNELL

Author of "Heart Lyrics"

"*A poet without love is a physical and metaphysical impossibility.*"—*Carlyle.*

SECOND SERIES

AMERICAN

NEW YORK AND LONDON

G. P. PUTNAM'S SONS

The Knickerbocker Press

INDEX OF AUTHORS, WITH CONTENTS.

For full Index of Subjects see end of Vol. II.

LOVE POEMS OF THREE CENTURIES

AMERICAN

LOVE POEMS OF THREE CENTURIES

AMERICAN

SAMUEL WOODWORTH.

IT is the very life and soul
  Of all that live, and breathe, and move ;
There 's not a pulse from pole to pole
  But vibrates solely from the power of love.
                                    Love.

LOVES SHE LIKE ME?

OH, say, my fluttering heart,
    Loves she like me ?
Is hers thy counterpart—
    Throbs it like thee ?
Does she remember yet
The spot where first we met,
Which I shall ne'er forget?
    Loves she like me ?

Soft echoes still repeat—
    " Loves she like me ? "
When on that mossy seat,
    Beneath the tree,

I wake my amorous lay,
While lambkins round me play,
And whispering zephyrs say,
Loves she like me?

On her I think by day,
  Loves she like me?
With her in dreams I stray,
  O'er mead and lea.
My hopes of earthly bliss
Are all comprised in this,
To meet her nuptial kiss,
  Loves she like me?

Does absence give her pain?
  Loves she like me?
And does she then arraign
  Fortune's decree?
Does she my name repeat?
Will she with rapture greet
The hour that sees us meet?
  Loves she like me?

WILLIAM CULLEN BRYANT.

MAIDENS' hearts are always soft ;
  Would that men's were truer !
                              Song.

THE BURIAL OF LOVE.

TWO dark-eyed maids, at shut of day,
  Sat where a river rolled away,
With calm sad brows and raven hair,
And one was pale and both were fair.

Bring flowers, they sang, bring flowers un-
    blown,
Bring forest-blooms of name unknown ;
Bring budding sprays from wood and wild,
To strew the bier of Love, the child.

Close softly, fondly, while ye weep,
His eyes, that death may seem like sleep,
And fold his hands in sign of rest,
His waxen hands, across his breast.

And make his grave where violets hide,
Where star-flowers strew the rivulet's side,
And bluebirds in the misty spring
Of cloudless skies and summer sing.

Place near him, as ye lay him low,
His idle shafts, his loosened bow,
The silken fillet that around
His waggish eyes in sport he wound.

But we shall mourn him long, and miss
His ready smile, his ready kiss,
The patter of his little feet,
Sweet frowns and stammered phrases sweet;

And graver looks, serene and high,
A light of heaven in that young eye,
All these shall haunt us till the heart
Shall ache and ache—and tears will start.

The bow, the band shall fall to dust,
The shining arrows waste with rust,
And all of Love that earth can claim,
Be but a memory and a name.

Not thus his nobler part shall dwell
A prisoner in this narrow cell;
But he whom now we hide from men,
In the dark ground, shall live again:

Shall break these clods, a form of light,
With nobler mien and purer sight,
And in the eternal glory stand,
Highest and nearest God's right hand.

RALPH WALDO EMERSON.

THE sense of the world is short,—
    Long and various the report,—
To love and be beloved ;
Men and gods have not outlearned it ;
And, how oft soe'er they 've turned it,
    'T is not to be improved.
Eros.

GIVE ALL TO LOVE.

GIVE all to love ;
    Obey thy heart ;
Friends, kindred, days,
Estate, good fame,
Plans, credit, and the Muse,—
Nothing refuse.

'T is a brave master ;
Let it have scope ;
Follow it utterly,
Hope beyond hope ;
High and more high
It dives into noon,
With wing unspent,
Untold intent ;

> But it is a god,
> Knows its own path,
> And the outlets of the sky.

> It was not for the mean ;
> It requireth courage stout,
> Souls above doubt,
> Valor unbending ;
> Such 't will reward,—
> They shall return
> More than they were,
> And ever ascending.

TO EVA.

O FAIR and stately maid, whose eyes,
    Were kindled in the upper skies
At the same torch that lighted mine ;
For so I must interpret still
Thy sweet dominion o'er my will,
    A sympathy divine.

Ah ! let me blameless gaze upon
Features that seem at heart my own ;
    Nor fear those watchful sentinels,
Who charm the more their glance forbids,
Chaste-glowing, underneath their lids,
    With fire that draws while it repels.

CHARLES FENNO HOFFMAN.

———

OH trust not Love, the wayward boy,
   But haste, if you 'd detain him,
Ere time can beauty's bond destroy,
Or other eyes and lips decoy,
   With Hymen to enchain him.
                              Trust not Love.

SONGS FROM " LOVE'S CALENDAR."

SHE loves, but 't is not me she loves,
   Not me on whom she ponders,
When in some dream of tenderness,
   Her truant fancy wanders.
The forms that flit her visions through
   Are like the shapes of old,
Where tales of Prince and Paladin
   On tapestry are told ;
Man may not hope her heart to win
   Be his of common mould.

But I—though spurs are won no more
   Where herald's trump is pealing,

Nor thrones carved out for lady fair
   Where steel-clad ranks are wheeling—
I loose the falcon of my hopes
   Upon as proud a flight
As they who hawked at high renown
   In song-ennobled fight.
If *daring*, then, true love may crown,
   My love she must requite !

———

Her heart is like a harp whose strings
   At will are touched by all ;
Her heart is like a bird that sings
   In answer to each fowler's call.
That harp !—has it one secret tone
Reserved for master-hands alone ?
That bird ! has it one soulful note
Which only toward its mate will float ?

Let it not wile thy soul away,
   That harp, with its beguiling touch ;
Let not that bird's bewildering lay
   Thrill through thy bosom overmuch ;
They 'll cheat thine eyes of sleep to-night,
Yet find thee dreaming with the light,
With heart and brain all idly stirred—
The music of that harp and bird !

The conflict is over, the struggle is past,
I have looked—I have loved—I have worshipped
    my last ;
And now back to the world, and let fate do her
    worst
On the heart that for thee such devotion has
    nursed.
To thee its best feelings were trusted away,
And life hath hereafter not one to betray.

Yet not in resentment thy love I resign ;
I blame not—upbraid not one motive of thine ;
I ask not what change has come over thy
    heart,
I reck not what chances have doomed us to part ;
I but know thou hast told me to love thee no
    more,
And I still must obey where I once did adore.

Farewell, then, thou loved one—oh ! loved but
    too well,
Too deeply, too blindly for language to tell—
Farewell ! thou hast trampled love's faith in
    the dust,
Thou hast torn from my bosom my hope and
    its trust !
But if thy life's current with bliss it would swell,
I would pour out my own in this last fond fare-
    well !

NATHANIEL PARKER WILLIS.

THEY may talk of love in a cottage,
   And bowers of trellised vine,
Of nature bewitchingly simple,
   And milkmaids half divine.

*   *   *   *   *   *

But give me a sly flirtation
   By the light of a chandelier—
With music to play in the pauses,
   And nobody very near.

Love in a Cottage.

STANZAS FROM " THE CONFESSIONAL."

I THOUGHT of thee—I thought of thee,
   On ocean many a weary night—
When heaved the long and solemn sea,
   With only waves and stars in sight.
We stole along by isles of balm,
   We furled before the coming gale,
We slept amid the breathless calm,
   We flew beneath the straining sail—
But thou wert lost for years to me,
And day and night I thought of thee.

I thought of thee—I thought of thee,
   In France—amid the gay saloon—

Where eyes as dark as eyes may be
  Are many as the leaves in June—
Where life is love, and even the air
  Is pregnant with impassioned thought.
And song and dance and music are
  With one warm meaning only fraught—
My half-snared heart broke lightly free,
And with a blush, I thought of thee.

* * * * * *

I 've thought of thee—I 've thought of thee
  Through change that teaches to forget ;
Thy face looks up from every sea,
  In every star thine eyes are set.
Though roving beneath Orient skies
  Whose golden beauty breathes of rest,
I envy every bird that flies
  Into the dark and clouded west ;
I think of thee—I think of thee !
O, dearest ! hast thou thought of me ?

THE ANNOYER.

LOVE knoweth every form of air,
  And every shape of earth,
And comes, unbidden, everywhere,
  Like thought's mysterious birth.
The moonlit sea and the sunset sky
  Are written with Love's words,
And you hear his voice unceasingly,
  Like song in the time of birds.

He peeps into the warrior's heart,
   From the tip of a stooping plume,
And the serried spears and the many men
   May not deny him room.
He 'll come to his tent in the weary night,
   And be busy in his dream ;
And he 'll float to his eye in morning light,
   Like a fay on a silver beam.

He hears the sound of the hunter's gun,
   And rides on the echo back,
And sighs in his ear, like a stirring leaf,
   And flits in the woodland track.
The shade of the wood, and the sheen of the
     river,
   The cloud and the open sky,
He will haunt them all with his subtle quiver,
   Like the light of your very eye.

The fisher hangs over the leaning boat,
   And ponders the silver sea,
For Love is under the surface hid,
   And a spell of thought has he.
He heaves the wave like a bosom sweet,
   And speaks in the ripple low,
Till the bait is gone from the crafty line,
   And the bare hook hangs below.

He blurs the print of the scholar's book,
  And intrudes in the maiden's prayer ;
And profanes the cell of the holy man,
  In the shape of a lady fair.
In the darkest night, and the bright daylight,
  In earth, and sea, and sky,
In every home of human thought,
  Will Love be lurking nigh.

HENRY WADSWORTH LONGFELLOW.

TALK not of wasted affection, affection never
    was wasted,
If it enrich not the heart of another, its waters,
    returning
Back to their springs, like the rain, shall fill
    them full of refreshment.

                                Evangeline.

SERENADE.

GOOD night ! good night, beloved !
    I come to watch o'er thee !
To be near thee—to be near thee,
  Alone is peace for me.

Thine eyes are stars of morning,
  Thy lips are crimson flowers !
Good night ! good night, beloved,
  While I count the weary hours.

ENDYMION.

THE rising moon has hid the stars ;
  Her level rays, like golden bars,
    Lie on the landscape green,
    With shadows long between.

And silver-white the river gleams,
As if Diana, in her dreams,
    Had dropt her silver bow
    Upon the meadows low.

On such a tranquil night as this,
She woke Endymion with a kiss,
    When, sleeping in the grove,
    He dreamed not of her love.

Like Dian's kiss, unasked, unsought,
Love gives itself, but is not bought ;
    Nor voice, nor sound betrays
    Its deep, impassioned gaze.

It comes,—the beautiful, the free,
The crown of all humanity,—
    In silence and alone,
    To seek the elected one.

It lifts the boughs, whose shadows deep
Are Life's oblivion, the soul's sleep,
    And kisses the closed eyes
    Of him who slumbering lies.

O weary hearts !   O slumbering eyes !
O drooping souls, whose destinies
  Are fraught with fear and pain,
  Ye shall be loved again !

No one is so accursed by fate,
No one so utterly desolate,
  But some heart, though unknown,
  Responds unto his own.

Responds,—as if with unseen wings,
An angel touched its quivering strings,
  And whispers, in its song,
  " Where hast thou stayed so long? "

JOHN GREENLEAF WHITTIER.

THE one great purpose of creation, Love,
  The sole necessity of earth and heaven.
                    Prelude to Among the Hills.

THE HENCHMAN.

MY lady walks her morning round,
    My lady's page her fleet greyhound,
My lady's hair the fond winds stir,
And all the birds make songs for her.

Her thrushes sing in Rathburn bowers,
And Rathburn side is gay with flowers;
But ne'er like hers, in flower or bird,
Was beauty seen or music heard.

The distance of the stars is hers;
The least of all her worshippers,
The dust beneath her dainty heel;
She knows not that I see or feel.

O proud and calm! she cannot know
Where'er she goes with her I go;
O cold and fair! she cannot guess
I kneel to share her hound's caress!

Gay knights beside her hunt and hawk,
I rob their ears of her sweet talk,
Her suitors come from east and west;
I steal her smiles from every guest.

Unheard of her, in loving words,
I greet her with the song of birds,
I reach her with her green-armed bowers,
I kiss her with the lips of flowers.

The hound and I are on her trail,
The wind and I uplift her veil;
As if the calm, cold moon she were,
And I the tide, I follow her.

As unrebuked as they, I share
The license of the sun and air,
And in a common homage hide
My worship from her scorn and pride.

World-wide apart, and yet so near,
I breathe her charmèd atmosphere,
Wherein to her my service brings
The reverence due to holy things.

Her maiden pride, her haughty name,
My dumb devotion shall not shame ;
The love that no return doth crave
To knightly levels lifts the slave.

No lance have I, in joust or fight
To splinter in my lady's sight ;
But, at her feet, how blest were I
For any need of hers to die !

OLIVER WENDELL HOLMES.

WHAT is a poet's love ?—
    To write a girl a sonnet,
To get a ring, or some such thing,
    And fustianize upon it.

The Poet's Lot.

THE STAR AND THE WATER-LILY.

THE sun stepped down from his golden throne
   And lay in the silent sea,
And the Lily had folded her satin leaves,
   For a sleepy thing was she ;
What is the Lily dreaming of ?
   Why crisp the waters blue ?
See, see, she is lifting her varnished lid !
   Her white leaves are glistening through.

The Rose is cooling his burning cheek
   In the lap of the breathless tide,—
The Lily hath sisters fresh and fair,
   That would lie by the Rose's side ;
He would love her better than all the rest,
   And he would be fond and true,—
But the Lily unfolded her weary lids,
   And looked at the sky so blue.

Remember, remember, thou silly one,
   How fast will thy summer glide,
And wilt thou wither a virgin pale,
   Or flourish a blooming bride ?
" O the Rose is old, and thorny, and cold,
   And he lives on earth," said she,
" But the Star is fair, and he lives in the air,
   And he shall my bridegroom be."

But what if the stormy cloud should come,
    And ruffle the silver sea?
Would he turn his eye from the distant sky,
    To smile on a thing like thee?
O no, fair Lily, he will not send
    One ray from his far-off throne ;
The winds shall blow and the waves shall flow,
    And thou wilt be left alone.

There is not a leaf on the mountain-top,
    Nor a drop of evening dew,
Nor a golden sand on the sparkling shore,
    Nor a pearl in the waters blue,
That he has not cheered with his fickle smile,
    And warmed with his faithless beam,—
And will he be true to a pallid flower,
    That floats on the quiet stream?

Alas for the Lily ! she would not heed,
    But turned to the skies afar,
And bared her breast to the trembling ray
    That shot from the rising star ;
The clouds came over the darkened sky,
    And over the waters wide ;
She looked in vain through the beating rain,
    And sank in the stormy tide.

STANZAS.

STRANGE ! that one lightly-whispered tone
  Is far, far sweeter unto me,
Than all the sounds that kiss the earth,
  Or breathe along the sea ;
But, lady, when thy voice I greet,
Not heavenly music seems so sweet.

I look upon the fair blue skies,
  And naught but empty air I see ;
But when I turn me to thine eyes,
  It seemeth unto me
Ten thousand angels spread their wings
Within those little azure rings.

The lily hath the softest leaf
  That ever western breeze hath fanned,
But thou shalt have the tender flower,
  So I may take thy hand ;
That little hand to me doth yield
More joy than all the broidered field,

O lady ! there may be many things
  That seem right fair, below, above ;
But sure not one among them all
  Is half so sweet as love ;—
Let us not pay our vows alone,
But join two altars both in one.

EDGAR ALLAN POE.

AND I lie so composedly
    Now in my bed,
(Knowing her love)
    That you fancy me dead ;
And I rest so contentedly
    Now in my bed
        (With her love at my breast),
    That you fancy me dead,—
That you shudder to look at me,
    Thinking me dead !
But my heart it is brighter
    Than all of the many
Stars in the sky ;
    For it sparkles with Annie—
It glows with the light
    Of the love of my Annie,
With the thought of the light
    Of the eyes of my Annie !

For Annie.

TO ONE IN PARADISE.

THOU wast that all to me, love,
    For which my soul did pine—
A green isle in the sea, love,
    A fountain and a shrine.

All wreathed with fairy fruits and flowers,
  And all the fruits were mine.

Ah, dream too bright to last !
  Ah, starry hopes that didst arise
But to be overcast !
  A voice from out the future cries,
"On ! on !"—but o'er the past
  (Dim gulf !) my spirit hovering lies,
Mute, motionless, aghast !

For alas ! alas ! with me
  The light of life is o'er !
No more—no more—no more—
  (Such language holds the solemn sea
To the sands upon the shore),
  Shall bloom the thunder-blasted tree,
Or the stricken eagle soar !

And all my days are trances,
  And all my nightly dreams
Are where thy dark eye glances,
  And where thy footstep gleams.
In what ethereal dances,
  By what ethereal streams !

ANNABEL LEE.

IT was many and many a year ago
   In a kingdom by the sea,
That a maiden lived, whom you may know
   By the name of Annabel Lee ;
And this maiden she lived with no other
    thought
   Than to love, and be loved by me.

I was a child, and she was a child,
   In this kingdom by the sea ;
But we loved with a love that was more than
    love,
   I and my Annabel Lee,—
With a love that the wingèd seraphs of heaven
   Coveted her and me.

And this was the reason that long ago,
   In this kingdom by the sea,
A wind blew out of a cloud, chilling
   My beautiful Annabel Lee ;
So that her high-born kinsmen came
   And bore her away from me,
To shut her up in a sepulchre,
   In this kingdom by the sea.

The angels, not so happy in heaven,
  Went envying her and me.
Yes ! that was the reason (as all men know)
  In this kingdom by the sea,
That the wind came out of the cloud by night,
  Chilling and killing my Annabel Lee.

But our love it was stronger by far than the
    love
  Of those who were older than we,
  Of many far wiser than we ;
And neither the angels in heaven above,
  Nor the demons down under the sea,
Can ever dissever my soul from the soul
  Of the beautiful Annabel Lee.

For the moon never beams without bringing
    me dreams
  Of the beautiful Annabel Lee,
And the stars never rise, but I feel the bright
    eyes
  Of the beautiful Annabel Lee ;
And so, all the night tide I lie down by the
    side
  Of my darling, my darling, my life, and my
    bride,
      In her sepulchre there by the sea,
      In her tomb by the sounding sea.

JOHN GODFREY SAXE.

MANLY strength is beauty's slave,
  And beauty yields to love.
              Hercules Spinning.

DARLING, TELL ME YES.

ONE little minute more, Maud,
  One little whisper more ;
I have a word to speak, Maud,
  I never breathed before.
What can it be but love, Maud ;
  And do I rightly guess
'T is pleasant to your ear, Maud ?
  O darling ! tell me yes !

The burden of my heart, Maud,
  There 's little need to tell ;
There 's little need to say, Maud,
  I 've loved you long and well.
There 's language in a sigh, Maud,
  One's meaning to express,
And yours—was it for me, Maud ?
  O darling ! tell me yes !

My eyes have told my love, Maud,
　And on my burning cheek,
You 've read the tender thought, Maud,
　My lips refused to speak.
I gave you all my heart, Maud,
　'T is needless to confess ;
And did you give me yours, Maud?
　O darling ! tell me yes !

'T is sad to starve a love, Maud,
　So worshipful and true ;
I know a little cot, Maud,
　Quite large enough for two ;
And you will be my wife, Maud?
　So may you ever bless
Through all your sunny life, Maud,
　The day you answered yes !

DO I LOVE THEE?

DO I love thee ?　Ask the bee
　　If she loves the flowery lea,
Where the honeysuckle blows
And the fragrant clover grows.
　As she answers, yes or no,
　Darling ! take my answer so.

Do I love thee?　Ask the bird
When her matin song is heard,

If she loves the sky so fair,
Fleecy cloud and liquid air.
  As she answers, yes or no,
  Darling ! take my answer so.

Do I love thee?   Ask the flower
If she loves the vernal shower,
Or the kisses of the sun,
Or the dew, when day is done.
  As she answers, yes or no,
  Darling ! take my answer so.

JOSIAH GILBERT HOLLAND.

IF love was lighted, oh, who can say ?—
  It was centuries ago—
And maids were the same in the olden day
  That they are now, I trow.

And who shall wonder, or who condemn—
  For their life had scanty zest—
If dangerous fancies came to them,
  As the men rode east and west ?
                    The Puritan's Guest.

LOVE'S PHILOSOPHIES.

A WIFE is like an unknown sea ;—
   Least known to him who thinks he knows
Where all the Shores of Promise be,
   Where lie the Islands of Repose,
And where the rocks that he must flee.

Capricious winds, uncertain tides,
   Drive the young sailor on and on,
Till all his charts and all his guides
   Prove false, and vain conceit is gone,
And only docile Love abides.

Where lay the shallows of the maid,
   No plummet-line the wife may sound,
Where round the sunny islands played,
   The pulses of the great profound,
Lies low the treacherous everglade.

And, as he sails, he is, perforce,
   Discoverer of a strange new world ;
And finds, whate'er may be his course,
   Green lands within white seas impearled
With streams of unsuspected source.

Which feed with gold delicious fruits
   Kept by unguessed Hesperides,

Or cool the lips of gentle brutes
  That breed and browse among the trees
Whose wind-tossed limbs and leaves are lutes.

The maiden free, the maiden wed,
  Can never, never be the same.
A new life springs from out the dead,
  And with the speaking of a name,
A breath upon the marriage bed,

She finds herself a something new—
  (Which he learns later, but no less),
And good or evil, false or true,
  May change their features—who can guess?-
Seen close, or on a nearer view.

For maiden life, with all its fire,
  Is hid within a grated cell,
Where every fancy and desire,
  And graceless passion, guarded well,
Sits dumb behind the woven wire.

Marriage is freedom : only when
  The husband turns the prison-key
Knows she herself, nor even then,
  Knows she more wisely well than he
Who finds himself least wise of men.

STANZAS FROM " DESPAIR."

AH ! what is so dead as a perished delight,
    Or a passion outlived ! or a scheme over
       thrown !
Save the bankrupt heart it has left in its flight,
    Still as quick as the eye, but as cold as a
       stone !

The honey-bee hoards for its winter-long need
    The treasure he gathers in joy from the flowers,
And drinks in each sip of its silvery mead
    The flavor and flush of the sweet summer
       hours.

But a pleasure expires at its earliest breath ;
    No labor can hoard it, no cunning can save ;
For the song of its life is the sigh of its death,
    And the sense it has thrilled is its shroud and
       its grave.

Ah ! what is our love, with its tincture of lust,
    And its pleasure that pains us and pain that
       endears,
But joy in an armful of beautiful dust
    That crumbles, and flies on the wings of the
       years ?

WILLIAM WETMORE STORY.

COME, as you came in the desert,
　　Ere we were women and men,
When the tiger passions were in us,
　　And love as you loved me then !
Cleopatra.

MARCUS ANTONIUS.

'TIS vain, Fonteus !　As the half-tamed steed,
　　Scenting the desert, lashes madly out,
And strains, and storms, and struggles to be
　　freed,
Shaking his rattling harness all about—
So, fiercer for restraint, here in my breast
Hot passion rages, firing every thought,
For what is honor, prudence, interest,
To the wild stress of love ?　Oh best of life,
My joy, hope, triumph, glory, my soul's wife,
My Cleopatra !　I desire thee so
That all restraint to the wild winds I throw,
Come what come will, come life, come death,
　　to me,
'T is equal, if again I look on thee.
Away, Fonteus ! tell her I rage
With madness for her.　Nothing can assuage

The strong desire, the torment, and fierce stress,
That whirls my thoughts round, and inflames
    my brain,
But her great ardent eyes—dark eyes that draw
My being to them with a subtle law
And an almost divine imperiousness.
Tell her I do not live until I feel
The thrill of her wild touch, that thro' each
    vein
Electric shoots its lightning ; and again
Hear those low tones of hers, although they
    steal,
As by some serpent-charm my will away,
And wreck my manhood.

      *   *   *   *   *   *

Tell my dear serpent I must see her to fill
My eyes with the glad light of her great eyes,
Though death, dishonor, any thing you will,
Stand in the way ! Ay, by my soul ! disgrace
Is better in the sun of Egypt's face,
Than pomp or power in this detested place.
Oh for the wine my queen alone can pour
From her rich nature ! Let me starve no more
On this weak, tepid drink that never warms
My life blood. But away with shams and forms !
Away with Rome ! One hour in Egypt's eyes
Is worth a score of Roman centuries.
Away, Fonteus ! Tell her till I see
Those eyes I do not live—that Rome to me

Is hateful,—tell her—Oh ! I know not what—
That every thought and feeling, space and spot,
Is like an ugly dream, where she is not.

*   *   *   *   *   *

Oh for a breath of Egypt !—the soft nights
In the voluptuous East—the dear delights
We tasted there—the lotus-perfumed gales
That dream along the low shores of the Nile,
And softly flutter in the languid sails !
Oh for the queen of all !—for the rich smile
That glows like autumn over her dark face—
For her large nature—her enchanting grace
Her arms, that are away so many a mile !
Away, Fonteus !—lose no hour—make sail—
Weigh anchor on the instant—woo a gale
To blow you to her. Tell her I shall be
Close on your very heels across the sea,
Praying that Neptune send me storms as strong
As passion is, to sweep me swift along,
Till the white spray sing whistling round my
       prow,
And the waves gurgle 'neath the keel's sharp
       plough.
Fly, fly, Fonteus ! When I think of her
My soul within my body is astir !
My wild blood pulses, and my hot cheeks glow !
Love with its madness overwhelms me so
That I—Oh ! go, I say ! Fonteus, go !

THE WALTZ.

MY arm is around your waist, love,
   Your hand is clasping mine,
Your head leans over my shoulder,
   As around in the waltz we twine.
I feel your quick heart throbbing,
   Your panting breath I breathe,
And the odor rare of your hyacinth hair
   Comes gently up from beneath.

To the rhythmic beat of the music,
   In the floating ebb and flow,
Of the tense violin, and the lisping flute,
   And the burring bass we go.
Whirling, whirling, whirling,
   In a rapture swift and sweet,
To the pleading violoncello's tones,
   And the pulsing piano's beat.

The world is alive with motion,
   The lights are whirling all,
And the feet and brain are stirred by the strain,
   Of the music's incessant call.
Dance! dance! dance! it calls to us,
   And borne on the waves of sound,
We circling swing in a dizzy ring,
   With the whole world whirling round.

The jewels dance on your bosom,
  On your arms the bracelets dance,
The swift blood speaks in your mantling cheeks,
  In your eyes is a dewy trance;
Your white robes flutter around you,
  Nothing is calm or still,
And the senses stir in the music's whir,
  With a swift electric thrill.

We pause, and your waist releasing,
  We stand and breathe for a while;
And, your face afire with a sweet desire,
  You look in my eyes and smile.
We scarcely can speak for panting,
  But I lean to you and say,
" Ah ! who, my love, can resist you ?
  You have waltzed my heart away."

JAMES RUSSELL LOWELL.

TRUE love is but a humble, low-born thing.
                                   Love.

PAOLO TO FRANCESCA.

I WAS with thee in heaven. I can not tell
  If years or moments, so the sudden bliss
When first we found, then lost us, in a kiss,
Abolished time, abolished earth and hell,

Left only heaven. Then from our blue there
    fell
A dagger's flash, and did not fall amiss,
For nothing now can rob my life of this—
That once with thee in Heaven, all else is well.
Us, undivided when man's vengeance came,
God's half-forgives that doth not here divide,
And, were this bitter whirl-blast fanged with
    flame,
To me, 't were summer, we being side by side :
This granted, I God's mercy would not blame,
For, given thy nearness, nothing is denied.

TELEPATHY.

" AND how could I dream of meeting?"
        Nay, how can you ask me sweet?
All day my pulse has been beating
    The tune of your coming feet.

And as nearer and ever nearer
    I felt the throb of your tread,
To be in the world grew dearer
    And my blood ran rosier red.

Love called, and I could not linger,
    But sought the forbidden tryst,
As music follows the finger
    Of the dreaming lutanist.

And though you had said it and said it,
  "We must not be happy to-day,"
Was I not wiser to credit
  The fire in my feet than your Nay?

WALT WHITMAN.

SOMETIMES with one I love I fill myself
    with rage for fear I effuse unreturned love,
But now I think there is no unreturned love, the
    pay is certain one way or another,
(I loved a certain person ardently and my love
    was not returned,
Yet out of that I have written these songs).

FAST ANCHORED, ETERNAL, O LOVE!

FAST-ANCHORED, eternal, O love! O wo-
    man I love!
O bride! O wife! more resistless than I can
    tell, the thought of you!
Then separate, as disembodied or another born,
Ethereal, the last athletic reality, my consola-
    tion,
I ascend, I float in the regions of your love,
    O man,
O sharer in my roving life.

AMONG THE MULTITUDE.

AMONG the men and women the multitude,
  I perceive one picking me out by secret
    and divine signs,
Acknowledging none else, not parent, wife,
    husband, brother, child, any nearer than
    I am,
Some are baffled, but that one is not—that one
    knows me.

Ah, lover and perfect equal,
I meant that you should discover me so by faint
    indirections,
And I, when I meet you, mean to discover you
    by the like in you.

ONCE I PASSED THROUGH A POPULOUS CITY.

ONCE I passed through a populous city im-
    printing my brain for future use with its
    shows, architecture, customs, traditions,
Yet now of all that city I remember only a
    woman I casually met there who detained
    me for love of me,
Day by day and night by night we were to-
    gether—all else has long been forgotten by
    me,

I remember, I say, only that woman who pas-
    sionately clung to me,
Again we wander, we love, we separate again,
Again she holds me by the hand, I must not go.
I see her close beside me with silent lips, sad
    and tremulous.

BENJAMIN FRANKLIN TAYLOR.

WHEN orchards drift with blooms of white
    like billows on the deep,
And whispers from the lilac bush across my
    senses sweep,
That 'mind me of a girl I knew when life was
    always May,
Who filled my nights with starry hopes that
    faded out by day.

October.

FROM "THE DESERTED HOMESTEAD."

FULL twenty summer-times ago,
    I walked along this country road,
When life and love were both in blow
    And none would dream it ever snowed.
        I saw a schoolma'am coming down,
        Her rippling hair was golden-brown,
        I saw her firm and slender hand,
        I saw her foot-prints in the sand.

A pair of rhymes in dainty type
  That brought to mind the old Gazette
Where village poets used to pipe—
  The cricket corner where they set,
    In little letters chirps of song
    Whose lines were only cricket long—
    And read them off as children tell
    A poem by the nonpareil.
I turned highwayman as I stood
  Beneath these oaks, now older grown,
And cried as ruder robbers would :
  " Thy life and treasure are my own ! "
    I halted her with love's surprise,
    And saw my answer in her eyes ;
    A bee was busy with a flower,
    A bird sang low from maple bower.
The old white school-house swarmed with noise ;
  We heeded not the babel rout,
The girls knew better than the boys
  What meant the meeting there without,
    And smiling stood and watched me hold
    Her hand in mine, and ran and told !

FROM "HEARTS AND HEARTHS."

THERE, couples sat the night away,
  Whist as a buttonhole bouquet—
Some russets roasting in a row,
Some talking flames that "told of snow,"
  Some cider that her hands had drawn,

Two pairs of lips, a single cup,
Both kissed the brim and drank it up.
  The candle has its night-cap on,
The very embers gone to bed—
Who shall record what either said?
Or, who so eloquent can tell
How early apples used to smell?
The woodsy, evanescent taste
Of berries plucked with eager haste,
As through the meadow-land they crept,
  And fingers touched and fancy woke
And never slumbered, never slept,
  Till day on life's sweet dreamings broke?
The pious clock a murmur made,
  Held up both hands before its face,
Not meant so much for twelve o'clock,
But just astonishment and shock
  At such a want of modest grace.
For up the sweetheart sprang, and laid
A muffling finger on the bell,
Lest the shrill steel should strike and tell,
And gave the hands a backward whirl,
Took time "on tick," the reckless girl!
Where is the lover? Old and lone.
And where the maiden? Gray and gone.
I read the dim *italic* stone :
A willow tree, a " Sacred To —— "
The sad old story, ever new,
For all the twain the world moves on.

FROM "THE MILLER AND THE MILL."

HE saw four butterflies winged in white,
   That fluttered over the wayside pool,
They look like bits of an old love-note
To Lucy Jones, and the first he wrote,
But never sent to the flower of school.
"What if he had?" and "Perhaps she might!"
He saw four butterflies winged in gold,
And thought what things the "perhaps" might
   fold :
A woman's foot on the powdered sill
With arch enough for a running rill,
To walk his world and—he thought again
How blossoms show in the route of rain—
Make summer-time till the first snow fall.
Perhaps and might ! How they puzzle all !

SINGLE POEMS.

PASSAGE FROM "THE WESTERN HOME."

HOW beautiful is woman's love !
   That from the play-place of its birth,
The sister's smile, the parent's hearth,
The earliest warmth of friendship true,

The holy church where first it knew
The balm of Christ's baptismal dew,
To stranger-bands, to stranger-home,
O'er desert clime, o'er ocean foam,

Goes forth in perfect trust, to prove
The untried toil, the burdening care,
The peril and the pang to dare.
Oh, glorious Love! whose purpose high
With guardian angel's constancy,
Till severing Death stands sternly by,
Hath to a mortal's keeping given
Its all of earth, its all of heaven.

Lydia Huntley Sigourney.

THE MATES.

THE bard has sung, God never formed a soul
    Without its own peculiar mate, to meet
Its wandering half, when ripe to crown the
    whole
    Bright plan of bliss, most heavenly, most
    complete.

But thousand evil things there are that hate
    To look on happiness : These hurt, impede,
And, leagued with time, space, circumstance,
    and fate,
    Keep kindred heart from heart, to pine and
    pant and bleed.

And, as the dove to far Palmyra flying
  From where her native founts of Antioch
    beam,
Weary, exhausted, longing, panting, sighing,
  Lights sadly at the desert stream ;

So many a soul o'er life's drear desert faring—
  Love's pure congenial spring unfound, un-
    quaffed—
Suffers, recoils, then, thirsting and despairing
  Of what it would, descends, and sips the
    nearest draught.

Maria Gowen Brooks.

A SERENADE.

LOOK out upon the stars, my love,
  And shame them with thine eyes,
On which, than on the lights above,
  There hang more destinies.
Night's beauty is the harmony
  Of blending shades and light,
Then, lady, up—look out, and be
  A sister to the night.

Sleep not !—thine image wakes for aye
  Within my watching breast ;

Sleep not !—from her soft sleep should fly
   Who robs all hearts of rest.
Nay, lady, from thy slumbers break,
   And make this darkness gay,
With looks whose brightness well might make
   Of darker night a day.

Edward Coate Pinkney.

HE MAY GO—IF HE CAN.

LET me see him once more, for a moment or
   two,
Let him tell me himself of his purpose, dear,
   do ;
Let him gaze in these eyes while he lays out
   his plan
To escape me, and then he may go—if he can.

Let me see him once more, let me give him
   one smile,
Let me breathe but one word of endearment
   the while.
I ask but that moment—my life on the man !
Does he think to forget me? He may—if he
   can.

Frances Sargent Osgood.

A GLIMPSE OF LOVE.

SHE came, as comes the summer wind,
  A gust of beauty to my heart ;
Then swept away, but left behind
  Emotions that shall not depart.

Unheralded she came and went,
  Like music in the silent night,
Which, when the burtheued air is spent,
  Bequeaths to memory its delight ;

Or, like the sudden April bow
  That spans the violet-waking rain,
She made those blessed flowers grow
  Which may not fall or fade again.

For sweeter than all things most sweet,
  And fairer than all things most fair,
She came and passed with footsteps fleet,
  A shining wonder in the air.

                    Thomas Buchanan Read.

MERCEDES.

UNDER a sultry, yellow sky,
　　On the yellow sand I lie ;
The crinkled vapors smite my brain,
I smoulder in a fiery pain.

Above the crags the condor flies,—
He knows where the red gold lies,
He knows where the diamonds shine :
If I knew, would she be mine ?

Mercedes in her hammock swings.—
In her court a palm-tree flings
Its slender shadow on the ground,
The fountain falls with silver sound.

Her lips are like this cactus cup,
With my hand I crush it up,
I tear its flaming leaves apart :—
Would that I could tear her heart !

Last night a man stood at her gate,
In the hedge I lay in wait ;
I saw Mercedes meet him there,
By the fire-flies in her hair.

I waited till the break of day,
Then I rose and stole away.
But left my dagger at her gate :—
Now she knows her lover's fate.

Elizabeth Stoddard.

4

DOES HE LOVE ME?

PRETTY robin at my window,
   Welcoming the day,
With thy loud and liquid piping,
   Read my riddle, pray.
I have conned it waking, sleeping,
   Vexed the more for aye,
Thou 'rt a wizard, pretty robin—
   Does he love me—say?

Lady violet, blooming meekly
   By the brooklet free,
Bending low thy gentle forehead
   All its grace to see.
Turn thee from the wooing water,
   Whisper soft, I pray,
For the winds might hear my secret—
   Does he love me—say?

Star that through the silent night-tide
   Watchest over him,
Write it with thy golden pencil
   On my casement dim.
Thou art skilled in love's sweet magic,
   Tell me, then, I pray,
Now, so none but I may read it—
   Does he love me—say?

Annie Chambers Ketchum.

SCENE FROM "PAOLO AND FRANCESCA."

Paolo—   I am mad !
The torture of unnumbered hours is o'er,
The strong cord has broken, and my heart
Riots in free delirium !   O Heaven !
I struggled with it, but it mastered me !
I fought against it, but it beat me down !
I prayed, I wept, but Heaven was deaf to me,
And every tear rolled backward on my heart
To blast and poison.

   Francesca—   And dost thou regret ?

   *Paolo—*The love ?   No, no ! I 'd dare it all
       again,
Its direst agonies, and meanest fears,
For that one kiss.   Away with fond remorse !
Here, on the brink of ruin, we two stand,
Lock hands with me, and brave the fearful
       plunge !
Thou canst not name a terror so profound
That I will look or falter from. Be bold.
I know thy love—I knew it long ago—
Trembled and fled from it.   But now I clasp
The peril to my breast, and ask of thee
A kindred desperation.

   Francesca (Throwing herself into his arms)—
Take me, all—
Body and soul !   The women of our clime

Do never give away but half a heart;
I have no part to give, part to withhold
In selfish safety.   When I saw thee first,
Riding alone amid a thousand men,
Sole in the lustre of thy majesty,
And Guido da Polenta said to me,
"Daughter, behold thy husband!"   With a
        bound
My heart went forth to meet thee.   He de-
        ceived.
He lied to me—ah! that 's the aptest word—
And I believed.   Shall I not turn again
And meet him craft with craft?   Paolo, love,
Thou 'rt dull—thou 'rt dying like a feeble fire
Before the sunshine.   Was it but a blaze,
A flash of glory, and a long, long night?
   Paolo—No, darling, no! you could not bend
        me back,
My course is onward, but my heart is sick with
        coming fears.
   Francesca—Away with them!   Must I
Teach thee to love? and reinform the ear
Of thy spent passion with some sorcery
To raise the chilly dead?
   Paolo—   Thy lips have not
A sorcery to rouse me as this spell.

                            [*Kisses her.*
   Francesca—I give thy kisses back to thee
        again,

And like a spendthrift only ask of thee
To take while I can give.
  Paolo—   Give, give, forever !
Have we not touched the height of human
        bliss ?
And if the sharp rebound may hurl us back
Among the prostrate, did we not soar once ?—
Taste heavenly nectar, banquet with the gods,
On high Olympus ? If they cast us, now,
Amid the furies, shall we not go down
With rich ambrosia clinging to our lips,
And richer memories settled in our hearts ?

George Henry Boker.

ANTONY TO CLEOPATRA.

I AM dying, Egypt, dying,
  Ebbs the crimson life-tide fast,
And the dark Plutonian shadows
  Gather on the evening blast ;
Let thine arms, O Queen, enfold me !
  Hush thy sobs and bow thine ear ;
Listen to the great heart-secrets,
  Thou, and thou alone, must hear.

Though my scarred and veteran legions
  Bear their eagles high no more,
And my wrecked and scattered galleys
  Strew dark Actium's fatal shore ;

Though no glittering guards surround me,
  Prompt to do their master's will,
I must perish like a Roman,
  Die the great Triumvir still.

Let not Cæsar's servile minions
  Mock the Lion thus laid low ;
'T was no foeman's arm that felled him—
  'T was his own that struck the blow,—
His, who, pillowed on thy bosom,
  Turned aside from glory's ray—
His, who, drunk with thy caresses,
  Madly threw a world away.

Should the base plebeian rabble
  Dare assail my name at Rome,
Where my noble spouse, Octavia,
  Weeps within her widowed home,
Seek her; say the gods bear witness—
  Altars, augurs, circling wings—
That her blood, with mine commingled,
  Yet shall mount the throne of kings.

And for thee, star-eyed Egyptian !
  Glorious sorceress of the Nile,
Light the path to Stygian horrors
  With the splendors of thy smile.

Give the Cæsar crowns and arches,
Let his brow the laurel twine ;
I can scorn the Senate's triumphs,
Triumphing in love like thine.

I am dying, Egypt, dying ;
Hark ! the insulting foeman's cry.
They are coming ! quick, my falchion !
Let me front them ere I die.
Ah ! no more amid the battle
Shall my heart exulting swell—
Isis and Orisis guard thee !
Cleopatra, Rome, farewell !

William Haines Lytle.

STANZAS FROM " AUNT HANNAH."

SHE was then a reigning belle, and I 've
heard old ladies tell
How at all the balls and parties Hannah
Amsden took the lead ;
Perfect bloom and maiden sweetness, lily grace
of rare completeness,
Though the stalk stands stiffly now the
flower has gone to seed.

She had all that love could give, all that makes
      it sweet to live—
  Fond caresses, jewels, dresses; and with
      eloquent appeal
Many a proud and rich adorer knelt—in meta-
      phor—before her;
  Metaphorically only does your modern lover
      kneel.

If she heeded, 't was because, in their worship,
      their applause,
  Her perfection was reflected, and a pleasing
      music heard;
But she suffered them no nearer than her gold-
      finch or her mirror,
  And she hardly held them dearer than her
      pier-glass or her bird.

But at last there came a day when she gave her
      heart away,
  If that rightly be called giving which is nei-
      ther choice nor will,
But a charm, a fascination, and a wild, sweet
      exultation—
  All the fresh young life outgoing in a strong
      ecstatic thrill.

At a city ball, by chance, she first met his ardent
      glance,
  He was neither young nor handsome, but a
      man of subtle parts,
With an eye of such expression as your lover
      by profession
  Finds an excellent possession when he goes
      a-hunting hearts.

It could trouble, it could burn ; and when first
      he chanced to turn
  That fine glance on Hannah Amsden, it lit up
      with swift desire,
With a sudden dilatation, and a radiant admira-
      tion,
  And shot down her soul's deep heaven like a
      meteor trailing fire.

How was any one to know that those eyes had
      looked just so
  On a hundred other women, with a gaze as
      bright and strange?
There are men who change their passions even
      oftener than their fashions ;
  And the best of loving always, to their minds,
      is still to change.

John T. Trowbridge.

JANET'S HAIR.

OH ! loosen the snood that you wear, Janet,
  Let me tangle a hand in your hair, my pet ;
For the world to me has no daintier sight
Than your brown hair behind your shoulders
    white,
As I tangled a hand in your hair, my pet.

It was brown, with a golden gloss, Janet,
It was finer than silk of the floss, my pet ;
  'T was a beautiful mist, falling down to your
    wrist ;
  'T was a thing to be braided, and jeweled and
    kissed ;
'T was the loveliest hair in the world, my pet.

My arm was the arm of a clown, Janet,
It was sinewy, bristled and brown, my pet ;
  But warmly and softly it loved to caress
  Your round white neck, and your wealth of
    tress,
Your beautiful plenty of hair, my pet.

Your eyes had a swimming gloss, Janet,
Revealing the dear old story, my pet !
  They were gray with that chastened tinge of
    the sky,

When the trout leaps quickest to snap the
    fly,
And they matched with your golden hair, my
    pet.

Your lips—but I have no words, Janet—
They were fresh as the twitter of birds, my
    pet ;
  When the Spring is young and the roses are
    wet
  With dewdrops in each bosom set,
And they suited your gold brown hair, my pet.

Oh ! you tangled my life in your hair, Janet !
'Twas a silken and golden snare, my pet ;
  But so gentle the bondage, my soul did im-
    plore
  The right to continue a slave evermore,
With my fingers enmeshed in your hair, my
    pet.

Thus ever I dream that you were, Janet,
With your lips, and your eyes, and your hair,
    my pet ;
  In the darkened and desolate years I moan,
  And my tears fall bitterly over the stone
That covers your golden hair, my pet.

Charles G. Halpine (*Miles O'Reilly*).

ALICE CARY.

O HEART of mine, what makes you beat
So fast and sweet, so fast and sweet?
A Spinster's Stint.

RUTH AND I.

IT was not day, and was not night;
The eve had just begun to light,
Along the lovely West,
His golden candles, one by one,
And girded up with clouds, the sun
Was sunken to his rest.

Between the furrows, brown and dry,
We walked in silence—Ruth and I,
We two had been, since morn
Began her tender tunes to beat
Upon the May leaves young and sweet,
Together, planting corn.

Homeward the evening cattle went,
In patient, slow, full-fed content,
Led by a rough, strong steer,
His forehead all with burs thick set,

His horns of silver tipt with jet,
  And shapeless shadow near.

With timid, half reluctant grace,
Like lovers in some favored place,
  The light and darkness met,
And the air trembled near and far,
With many a little tuneful jar
  Of milk-pans being set.

We heard the house-maids at their cares
Pouring their hearts out unawares
  In some sad poet's ditty,
And heard the fluttering echoes round
Reply like souls all softly drowned
  In heavenly love and pity.

All sights, all sounds, in earth and air,
Were of the sweetest ; everywhere
  Ear, eye, and heart were fed :
The grass with one small burning flower
Blushed bright, as if the elves that hour
  Their coats thereon had spread.

One moment, where we crossed the brook,
Two little sunburnt hands I took,—
  Why did I then let go?
I 've been since then in many a land,
Touched, held, kissed many a fairer hand,
  But none that thrilled me so.

Why, when the bliss heaven for us made
Is in our very bosoms laid,
 Should we be all unmoved,
And walk, as now do Ruth and I,
'Twixt th' world's furrows, brown and dry,
 Unloving and unloved?

PRODIGAL'S PLEA.

SHINE down, little head, so fair,
 From thy window in the wall ;
Oh, my slighted golden hair,
 Like the sunshine round me fall—
Little head, so fair, so bright,
Fill my darkness with thy light !

Reach me down thy helping hand,
 Little sweetheart, good and true ;
Shamed, and self-condemned, I stand,
 And wilt thou condemn me too?
Soilure of sin, be sure,
Cannot harm thy hand so pure.

With thy quiet, calm my cry
 Pleading to thee from afar.
Is it not enough that I
 With myself should be at war?
With thy cleanness cleanse my blood,
With thy goodness make me good.

Eyes that loved me once, I pray,
  Be not crueller than death,
Hide each sharp-edged glance away
  Underneath its tender sheath !
Make me not, sweet eyes, with scorn,
Mourn that I was ever born !

Oh, my roses ! are ye dead,
  That in love's delicious day,
Used to flower out ripe and red,
  Fast as kisses plucked away ?
Turn thy pale cheek, little wife,
Let me warm them back to life.

I have wandered, oh, so far !
  From the way of truth and right ;
Shine out for my guiding star,
  Little head, so dear and bright,
Dust of sin is on my brow,
Good enough for both art thou !

PHŒBE CARY.

" LOVE thee ? " Thou canst not ask of me
  So freely as I fain would give,
'T is woman's great necessity
  To love as long as she shall live.
A Woman's Answer.

SONG.

LAUGH out, O stream, from your bed of green,
 Where you lie in the sun's embrace;
And talk to the weeds that o'er you lean
 To touch your dimpled face;
But let your talk be sweet as it will,
 And your laughter be as gay,
You cannot laugh as I laugh in my heart,
 For my lover will come to-day.

Sing sweet, little bird, sing out to your mate
 That hides in the leafy grove;
Sing clear and tell him for him you wait,
 And tell him of all your love;
But though you sing till you shake the buds
 And the tender leaves of May,
My spirit thrills with a sweeter song,
 For my lover must come to-day.

Come up, O winds, come up from the south,
 With eager, hurrying feet,
And kiss your red rose on her mouth
 In the bower where she blushes sweet;
But you cannot kiss your darling flower,
 Though you clasp her as you may,
As I kiss in thought the lover dear
 I shall hold in my arms to-day!

HELPLESS.

YOU never said a word to me
  That was cruel under the sun ;
It is n't the things you do, darling,
  But the things you leave undone.

If you could know a wish or want,
  You would grant it joyfully ;
Ah ! that is the worst of all, darling,
  That you cannot know nor see.

For favors free alone are sweet,
  Not those that we must seek ;
If you loved me as I love you, darling,
  I would not need to speak.

But to-day I am helpless as a child
  That must be led along ;
Then put your hand in mine, darling,
  And make me brave and strong !

There 's a heavy care upon my mind,
  A trouble on my brain ;
Now gently stroke my hair, darling,
  And take away the pain.

5

I feel a weight within my breast,
    As if all had gone amiss ;
Oh, kiss me with thy lips, darling,
    And fill my heart with bliss !

Enough ! no deeper joy than this
    For souls below is given ;
Now take me in your arms, darling,
    And lift me up to heaven !

THOMAS WENTWORTH HIGGINSON.

O PASSIONATE earthly love,
    Whose tremulous pulse beats on to life's
      best boon,
Couldst thou not give one noon,
One noon of noons, all other bliss above ?
                A Song of Days.

SERENADE BY THE SEA.

O'ER the ocean vague and wide
    Sleep comes with the coming tide.
Breezes lull my lady fair,
Cool her eyelids, soothe her hair,
While the murmuring surges seem
To float her through a world of dream.

Shadowy sloops are gliding in
Safe the harbor-bar within.
Silently each phantom pale
Drops the anchor, furls the sail.
She, meanwhile, remote from me,
Drifts on sleep's unfathomed sea.

So may every dream of ill
Find its anchorage, and be still ;
Sorrow furl its sails and cease
In this midnight realm of peace,
And each wandering thought find rest
In the haven of her breast.

"SINCE CLEOPATRA DIED."

"SINCE Cleopatra died!" Long years are
    past,
In Antony's fancy, since the deed was done.
Love counts in epochs, not from sun to sun,
But by the heart throb. Mercilessly fast
Time has swept onward since she looked her last
On life, a queen. For him the sands have run
Whole ages through their glass, and kings have
    won
And lost their empires o'er earth's surface vast

Since Cleopatra died. Ah ! Love and Pain
Make their own measure of all things that be.

No clock's slow ticking marks their deathless
  strain ;
The life they own is not the life we see ;
Love's single moment is eternity ;
Eternity a thought in Shakespeare's brain.

RICHARD HENRY STODDARD.

AND then was she aware of, first
  That she, not knowing it, had nursed
His memory till it grew a part—
A heart within her very heart.

Leonatus.

THE TURKISH MAIDEN.

IF you meet my sweet gazelle,
  By these signs you 'll know her well ;
Eyes like arrows, black and bright,
Cheeks the fiery rose of night,
And her voice a silver bell.

I am burning with desire,
Like a parchment in the fire ;
I am dying ; hear my cry,
'T is for thee alone I sigh,
Emir's Daughter—Peacock's Eye !

Heart of rocks ! be soft to me,
Or my tears will soften thee—
In my passion and my pain
Flowing down my cheeks like rain—
And they will not flow in vain !

I know where her palace stands,
It is in the far-off lands,
Over mountains, over sands :
Seldom letters reach her there,
Never wretched lover's prayer !

I am dying, for no art
Can relieve my broken heart.
What I suffer none can tell,
Blasted by the fires of hell—
By the love of that gazelle !

There 's a stately palm that grows
Where the purest water flows :
She 's its fruit : her lips are red
As the blush that rubies shed,
Or the west when day is dead !

Life and death are met in me,
But I only think of thee.
Let the happy fool complain,
What is dying ? Where 's the pain ?
I have lived and loved in vain !

LOVE THY NEIGHBOR.

" LOVE thy neighbor as thyself."
   When at dawn I meet her,
As by the garden wall she stands,
   And gives me flowers across the wall,
My heart goes out to kiss her hands—
   Are hands or flowers the sweeter?—
I 'm ready at her feet to fall,
   And like a clown to labor !
Better than I love myself
   Do I love my neighbor !

" Love thy neighbor as thyself."
   When at dawn I meet him,
As by the garden wall he stands,
   And takes my flowers across the wall,
My soul 's already in his hands—
   It flew so fast to greet him !
And O, I grow so proud and tall,
   And my heart beats like a tabor !
Better than I love myself
   Do I love my neighbor !

SONG.

I KNOW a little rose,
   And O, but I were blest
Could I but be the drop of dew
   That lies upon her breast!

But I dare not look so high,
   Nor die a death so sweet;
It is enough for me to be
   The dust about her feet!

BAYARD TAYLOR.

O FLUTTERING heart! control thy
      tumult
Lest eyes profane should see
My cheeks betray the rush of rapture
   Her coming brings to me!

The Phantom.

TRUE LOVE'S TIME OF DAY.

WHEN shall I find you, sweetheart,
   That shall be and must be mine?
I seek, though the world divide us,
   And I send you the secret sign.

There 's blood in the veins of morning,
    So fresh it may well deceive,
When man goes forth as Adam,
    And woman awaits him as Eve.

There 's an elvish spell in twilight,
    When the bats of fancy fly,
And sense is bound by a question
    And Fate in the quick reply.

And the moon is an old enchantress,
    With her snares of glimmer and shade,
That have ever been false and fatal
    To the dreams of man and maid.

But I 'll meet you at noonday, sweetheart,
    In the billowy fields of grain,
When the sun is hot for harvest
    And the roses athirst for rain.

With the daylight's truth on your forehead,
    And the daylight's love in your eye,
And I 'll kiss you without question,
    And you 'll kiss me without reply.

IF LOVE SHOULD COME AGAIN.

IF Love should come again, I ask my heart,
　In tender tremors, not unmixed with pain,
Couldst thou be calm, nor feel thy ancient smart,
　　If Love should come again?

Couldst thou unbar the chambers where his nest
　So long was made, and made, alas! in vain,
Nor with embarrassed welcome chill the guest,
　　If Love should come again?

Would Love his ruined quarters recognize
　Where shrouded pictures of the past remain,
And gently turn them with forgiving eyes,
　　If Love should come again?

Would bliss, in milder type, spring up anew,
　As silent craters with the scarlet stain
Of flowers repeat the lava's ancient hue,
　　If Love should come again?

Would Fate, relenting, sheathe the cruel blade
　Whereby the angel of thy youth was slain,
That thou might'st all possess him, unafraid,
　　If Love should come again?

In vaiu I ask.   My heart makes no reply,
But echoes evermore the sweet refrain,
Till, trembling lest it seem a wish, I sigh,
If Love should come again !

JULIA C. R. DORR.

BUT I pray you think when some fairer face
Shines like a star from her wonted place,
That love will starve if it is not fed,
That true hearts pray for their daily bread.
A Flower for the Dead.

FORESHADOWINGS.

WIND of the winter night,
Under the starry skies
Somewhere my lady bright,
Slumbering lies.
Wrapped in calm maiden dreams,
Where the pale moonlight streams,
Softly she sleeps.

I do not know her face,
Pure as the lonely star
That in yon darkling space
Shineth afar ;

Never with soft command
Touched I her willing hand,
        Kissed I her lips.

I have not heard her voice,
        I do not know her name ;
Yet doth my heart rejoice,
        Owning her claim ;
Yet am I true to her ;
All that is due to her
        Sacred I keep.

Never a thought of me
        Troubles her soft repose ;
Courant of mine may be
        Lily nor rose.
They may not bear to her
This heart's fond prayer to her,
        Yet—she is mine.

Wind of the winter night,
        Over the fields of snow,
Over the hills so white,
        Tenderly blow !
Somewhere red roses bloom ;
Into her warm, hushed room,
        Bear thou their breath.

Whisper—Nay, nay, thou sprite,
        Breathe thou no tender word ;

Wind of the winter night,
   Die thou unheard.
True love shall yet prevail,
Telling his own sweet tale :
   Till then I wait.

WON.

BIRD, by her garden gate
   Singing thy happy song,
Round thee the listening leaves
   Joyously throng.
Tell them that yesternight
Under the stars so bright,
   I wooed and won her !

Red rose, rejoice with me !
   Swing all thy censers low,
Bid each fair bud of thine
   Hasten to blow.
Lift every glowing cup
Brimming with sweetness up,
   For—I have won her !

Wind, bear the tidings far,
   Far over hill and dale ;
Let every breeze that blows

Swell the glad tale.
River, go tell the sea,
Boundless and glad and free,
    That I have won her!

Stars, ye who saw the blush
    Steal o'er her lovely face,
When first her tender lips
    Granted me grace,
Who can with her compare,
Queen of the maiden's rare?
    Yet—I have won her!

Sun, up yon azure height
    Treading thy lofty way,
Ruler of sea and land,
    King of the Day—
Where 'er thy banners fly,
Who is so blest as I?
    I—who have won her?

Oh, heart and soul of mine,
    Make ye the temple clean,
Make all the cloisters pure,
    Seen and unseen!
Bring fragrant balm and myrrh,
Make the shrine meet for her,
    Now ye have won her!

LUCY LARCOM.

L OVE, sin-touched, is an unwholesome thing,
   A growth reversed, blight clinging into
     blight;
Love meant to hallow all things with its light!
               Why Life is Sweet.

BESSIE AND RUTH.

A BOVE them, the meadow-lark's call
   Rose, piercing the tremulous ether,
As they clambered across the stone wall,
  And came home through the lane together.
    Two girls, in their gowns of blue,
    With their milking-pails came through
Red waves of the wind-shaken clover;
    And the bloom of the grass dropped dew,
    And the dawn into sunrise grew,
As they loitered talking it over—
Talking a love-secret over.

Their secret; they thought it was hid,
  But the wren and the bobolink knew it;
And a wood-thrush, the alders amid,
  To his mate in a flute-echo threw it;
    They talked of two lads on the sea,
    They talked of two weddings to be;

And a rose-colored future each wove her ;
    Two hearts that were fettered, though
        free,—
    In the shade of a green-golden tree,
As they lingered, talking it over,—
Talking the old story over.

They climbed the bleak slopes of a cliff
  Made warm by the footsteps of summer,
And each asked the solemn waves if
  They had heard of a laggard home-comer.
    Mist-flushed with the heats of July,
    The white, solemn vessels went by,
But neither saw sign of her rover !
    And the deeps of Ruth's dreamy blue eye
    Were ruffled by Bessie's long sigh,
While the slow waves murmured it over—
Murmured the mystery over.

They parted at dusk on the beach ;
  The third moon of harvest was waning,
A yearning was in their low speaking,
  As of billow to billow complaining.
    To Bessie, the deep faith of Ruth
    Lapsed sad as the ebb-tide of youth ;
And the stars in the sky-gulf above her
    Sank chill as her dumb thoughts in sooth,
    For she doubted her own maiden truth,

Dreaming another love over—
Wondering, dreaming it over.

The lark's note pierced Heaven again ;
  And again, in the June-lighted weather,
The footsteps of two down the lane
  Kept time to a love-tune together.
    The gossip of bluebird and thrush
    Slid lightly from tree-top to bush,
And shook with faint laughter the clover ;
    And the sweet-brier bent with a blush,
    That warned the pert blackbird to hush,
While Bessie went by with her lover,
Talking her second love over.

Ruth came through the brown fields alone,
  To the sea, veiled in gray of November ;
Dead leaves rustled past ; with a moan
  Strove the wind to revive autumn's ember.
    But the youth-light shone in her eye,
    And a joy in her heart, sweet and high,
Sang clearer than curlew or plover.
    There is hope that is never put by !
    There is love that refuses to die!
And the old sea this burden croons over,
Forever over and over.

ROSE TERRY COOKE.

FOR love with loving is not spent,
  Not such is love's divine intent ;
What year on year the sun shall dim ?
What worship tire the seraphim ?
                              An Answer.

HE AND SHE.

HOW does a woman love ?   Once, no more,
  Though life forever its loss deplore.
Deep in sorrow, or want, or sin,
One king reigneth her heart within ;
One alone, by night and day,
Moves her spirit to curse or pray ;
One voice only can call her soul
Back from the grasp of death's control ;
Though loves beset her and friends deride ;
Yea, when she smileth another's bride ;
Still for her master her life makes moan ;
Once is forever, and once alone.

How does a man love ?   Once for all ;
The sweetest voices of life may call,
Sorrow daunt him, or death dismay,
Joy's red roses bedeck his way,

Fortune smile or jest or frown,
The cruel thumb of the world turn down,
Loss betray him, or gain delight,
Through storm or sunshine, by day or night,
Wandering, toiling, asleep, awake,
Though souls may madden or frail hearts
    break ;
Better than wife, or child, or pelf,
Once and forever, he loves—himself!

ONCE BEFORE.

SOLE she sat beside her window,
  Hearing only raindrops pour,
  Looking only at the shore,
When, outside the little casement,
Weeping in a feigned abasement,
  Love stood knocking—
Knocking at her bolted door.

Slow she swung the little casement
  Where the autumn roses glowed,
  Sweet and sad her deep eyes showed ;
And her voice, in gentlest measure,
Said aloud—" Nor Love, nor Pleasure,
  Can come in here any more—
Never any more ! "

" But I am not Love or Pleasure—
I am but an orphan baby ;
Lost my mother is, or maybe
Dead she lies, while I am weeping,"
Sobbed the child, his soft lie creeping
Softly through the bolted door—
Through the maiden's door.

Low she said, in accents lonely :
" Once I let him in before,
Once I opened wide my door.
Ever since my life is dreary,
All my prayers are vague and weary ;
Once I let him in before,
Now I 'll double-lock the door."

In the rain he stands imploring,
Tears and kisses storm the door,
Where she let him in before,
Will she never know repenting ?
Will she ever, late relenting,
Let him in, as once before ?
Will she double-lock the door ?

PAUL HAMILTON HAYNE.

LOVE scorns degrees : the low he lifteth high,
   The high he draweth down to that fair plain
Whereon, in his divine equality,
Two loving hearts may meet.
        The Mountain of the Lovers.

DEAD LOVES.

WHENE'ER I think of old loves wan and
   dead,
Of passion's wine outpoured in senseless dust,
Of doomed affections and long-buried trust,
Through all my soul an arctic gloom is shed ;
And, oh ! I walk the world disquieted.
Thou, my own love ! white lily of April ! Must
Thy beauty, perfume, radiance, all be thrust
Earthward, to crumble in a grass-grown bed ?
Yea, sweet, t is even so ! How long, how long,
The dust of her who once was tender Ruth
Hath mouldered dumbly ! And how oft the
   clod
Which binds, like hers, all perished love and
   truth,
Strives with pale weeds to veil death's hopeless
   wrong,
Or through chill lips of flowers appeals to God !

LOVE'S AUTUMN.

TO MY WIFE.

I WOULD not lose a single silvery ray
  Of those white locks which like a milky way
Streak the dusk midnight of thy raven hair ;

I would not lose, O sweet ! the misty shine
Of those half-saddened, thoughtful eyes of
    thine,
Whence Love looks forth, touched by the
    shadow of care ;

I would not miss the droop of thy dear mouth,
The lips less dewy-red than when the South—
The young South wind of passion sighed o'er
    them ;

I would not miss each delicate flower that
    blows
On thy wan cheeks, soft as September's rose
Blushing but faintly on its faltering stem ;

I would not miss the air of chastened grace
Which breathed divinely from thy patient face,
Tells of love's watchful anguish, merged in
    rest ;

Naught would I miss of all thou hast, and art,
O! friend supreme, whose constant, stainless
　　heart
Doth house, unknowing, many an angel guest ;

Their presence keeps thy spiritual chambers
　　pure ;
While the flesh fails, strong love grows more
　　and more
Divinely beautiful with perished years ;

Thus, at each slow, but surely deepening sign
Of life's decay, we will not, Sweet ! repine,
Nor greet its mellowing close with thankless
　　tears ;

Love's spring was fair, love's summer brave and
　　bland,
But through love's autumn mist I view the land,
The land of deathless summers yet to be ;

There I behold thee, young again and bright,
In a great flood of rare transfiguring light,
But there as here, thou smilest, Love, on me !

HELEN HUNT JACKSON

"H. H."

AH, they know not heart
  Of man or woman who declare
That love needs time to love and dare.
His altars wait,—not day nor name,
Only the touch of sacred flame.

The Story of Boon.

A ROSE-LEAF.

A ROSE-LEAF on the snowy deck;
  The high wind whirling it astern;
Nothing the wind could know or reck;
  Why did the king's eyes thither turn?

"The queen hath walked here!" hoarse he cried.
    The courtiers, stunned, turned red, turned
      white;
No use if they had stammered, lied;
  Aghast they fled his angry sight.

King's wives die quick, when kings go mad;
  To death how fair and grave she goes!
What if the king knew now she had
  Shut in her hand a little rose?

And men die quick when kings have said ;
 Bleeding, dishonored, flung apart
In outcast field a man lies dead,
 With rose-leaves warm upon his heart.

BURNT SHIPS.

O LOVE, sweet Love, who came with rosy sail
 And foaming prow across the misty sea !
O Love, brave Love, whose faith was full and
 free
That lands of sun and gold, which could not fail
Lay in the west, that bloom no winter gale
Could blight, and eyes whose love thine own
 should be,
Called thee, with steadfast voice of prophecy,
To shores unknown !

 O Love, poor Love, avail
Thee nothing now thy faiths, thy braveries ;
There is no sun, no bloom ; a cold wind strips
The bitter foam from off the wave where dips
No more thy prow ; the eyes are hostile eyes ;
The gold is hidden ; vain thy tears and cries ;
O Love, poor Love, why didst thou burn thy
 ships ?

TOGETHER.

NO touch—no sight—no sound—wide conti-
    nents
And seas clasp hands to separate
Them from each other now. Too late!
Triumphant love has leagued the elements
To do their will. Hath light a mate
For swiftness? Can it overweight
The air? Or doth the sun know accidents?
The light, the air, the sun, inviolate
For them, do constant keep and state
Message of their ineffable contents
And raptures, each in each. So great
Their bliss of loving, even fate,
In parting them, hath found no instruments
Whose bitter pain insatiate
Doth kill it, or their faith abate
In presence of love's hourly sacraments.

A WOMAN'S DEATH-WOUND.

IT left upon her tender flesh no trace.
    The murderer is safe. As swift as light
The weapon fell, and, in the summer night,
Did scarce the silent, dewy air displace;
'T was but a word. A blow had been less base.
Like dumb beast, branded by an iron white

With heat, she turned in blind and helpless
    flight,
But then remembered, and with piteous face
    came back.
Since then, the world has nothing missed
In her, in voice, or smile.   But she—each day
She counts until her dying be complete.
One moan she makes, and ever doth repeat :
" O lips that I have loved and kissed and
    kissed,
Did I deserve to die this bitterest way ? "

ELIZABETH AKERS ALLEN.

" FLORENCE PERCY."

YOU did not see the bitter trace
  Of anguish sweep across my face ;
You did not hear my proud heart beat,
Heavy and slow beneath your feet ;
You thought of triumphs still unwon,
Of glorious deeds as yet undone ;
And I, the while you talked to me,
I watched the gulls float lonesomely,
Till lost amid the hungry blue,
And loved you better than you knew.
Left Behind.

WITH THEE.

IF I could know that after all
  These heavy bonds have ceased to thrall,
    We, whom in life the fates divide,
    Should sweetly slumber side by side—
That one green spray would drop its dew
Softly alike above us two,
      All would be well, for I should be
      At last, dear loving heart, with thee !

How sweet to know this dust of ours,
Mingling, will feed the self-same flowers,—
    The scent of leaves, the song-bird's tone,
    At once across our rest be blown,—
One breadth of sun, one sheet of rain
Make green the grass above us twain !
      Ah, sweet and strange, for I should be,
      At last, dear tender heart, with thee !

But half the earth may intervene
Thy place of rest and mine between—
    And leagues of land and wastes of waves
    May stretch and toss between our graves—
Thy bed with summer light be warm
While snow-drifts heap, in wind and storm,
      My pillow, whose one thorn will be,
      Beloved, that I am not with thee !

But if there be a blissful sphere
Where homesick souls, divided here,
    And wandering wide in useless quest,
    Shall find their longed-for heaven of rest,—
If in that higher, happier birth
We meet the joy we missed on earth,
    All will be well, for I shall be,
    At last, dear loving heart, with thee !

THE SILVER BRIDGE.

THE sunset fades along the shore,
    And faints behind yon rosy reach of sea
Night falls again, but oh, no more,
      No more, no more,
    My love returns to me.
The lonely moon builds soft and slow
Her silver bridge across the main,
    But him who sleeps the wave below,
      Love waits in vain,
        Ah no, ah no,
He never comes again !

But while some night beside the sea
I watch, when sunset's red has ceased to burn,
    That silver path, and sigh, " Ah me,
      Ah me, ah me,
    He never will return ! "
If on that bridge of rippling light,
His homeward feet should find their way,

I should not wonder at the sight,
But only say :
"Ah love, my love,
I knew you would not stay ! "

GOING TO SLEEP.

THE light is fading down the sky,
The shadows grow and multiply,
I hear the thrush's evening song ;
But I have borne with toil and wrong
So long, so long !
Dim dreams my drowsy senses drown,—
So, darling, kiss my eyelids down !

My life's brief spring went wasted by,—
My summer ended fruitlessly ;
I learned to hunger, strive, and wait,—
I found you, love,—oh, happy fate !—
So late, so late !
Now all my fields are turning brown,—
So, darling, kiss my eyelids down !

Oh, blessèd sleep !   Oh, perfect rest !
Thus pillowed on your faithful breast,
Nor life nor death is wholly drear,
O tender heart, since you are here,
So dear, so dear !
Sweet love, my soul's sufficient crown !
Now, darling, kiss my eyelids down !

EDMUND CLARENCE STEDMAN.

———

PERHAPS 't was boyish love, yet still,
    O listless woman, weary lover !
To feel once more that fresh, wild thrill
    I 'd give—but who can live youth over ?

The Doorstep.

ESTELLE.

OF all the beautiful demons who fasten on
    human hearts,
To fetter the bodies and souls of men with ex-
    quisite mocking arts,
The cruellest, and subtlest, and fairest to mortal
    sight
Is surely a woman called Estelle, who tortures
    me day and night.

The first time that I saw her she passed with
    sweet lips mute,
As if in scorn of the vacant praise of those who
    made her suit ;
A hundred lustres flashed and shone as she
    rustled through the crowd,
And a passion seized me for her there,—so
    passionless and proud.

The second time that I saw her she met me face
    to face,
Her bending beauty answered my bow in a
    tremulous moment's space ;
With an upward glance that instantly fell, she
    read me through and through,
And found in me something worth her while to
    idle with and subdue ;

Something, I know not what ; perhaps the spirit
    of eager youth
That named her a queen of queens, at once, and
    loved her in very truth ;
That threw its pearl of pearls at her feet, and
    offered her, in a breath,
The costliest gift a man can give from his cradle
    to his death.

The third time that I saw her—this woman
    called Estelle—
She passed her milk-white arm through mine
    and dazzled me with her spell ;
A blissful fever thrilled my veins, and there, in
    the moon-beams white,
I yielded my soul to the fierce control of that
    maddening delight !

And at many a trysting afterwards she wove my
    heart-strings round

Her delicate fingers, twisting them, and chant-
  ing low as she wound ;
The tune she sang rang sweet and clear like the
  chime of a witch's bell ;
Its echo haunts me even now, with the word,
  Estelle ! Estelle !

Ah, then, as a dozen before me had, I lay at last
  at her feet,
And she turned me off with a calm surprise when
  her triumph was all complete :
It made me wild, the stroke which smiled so
  pitiless out of her eyes,
Like lightning fallen, in clear noonday, from
  cloudless and bluest skies !

The whirlwind followed upon my brain and beat
  my thoughts to rack.
Who knows how many a month I lay ere mem·
  ory floated back ?
Even now, I tell you, I wonder whether this
  woman called Estelle
Is flesh and blood, or a beautiful lie sent up
  from the depths of hell.

For at night she stands where the pallid moon
  streams into this grated cell,
And only gives me that mocking glance when
  I speak her name—Estelle.

With the old resistless longing often I strive to
    clasp her there,
But she vanishes from my open arms and hides
    I know not where.

And I hold that if she were human she could
    not fly like the wind,
But her heart would flutter against my own in
    spite of her scornful mind :
Yet, oh ! she is not a phantom, since devils are
    not so bad
As to haunt and torture a man long after their
    tricks have made him mad !

THE WEDDING-DAY.

I.

SWEETHEART, name the day for me
    When we two shall wedded be.
Make it ere another moon,
While the meadows are in tune,
And the trees are blossoming,
And the robins mate and sing ;
Whisper, love, and name a day
In this merry month of May.

No, no, no,
You shall not escape me so !
Love will not forever wait ;
Roses fade when gathered late.

7

II.

Fie, for shame, Sir Malcontent !
How can time be better spent
Than in wooing?   I would wed
When the clover blossoms red,
When the air is full of bliss,
And the sunshine like a kiss.
If you 're good I 'll grant a boon.
You shall have me, sir, in June.

Nay, nay, nay,
Girls for once should have their way !
If you love me wait till June ;
Rosebuds wither picked too soon.

HARRIET PRESCOTT SPOFFORD.

TWO faces bent,—
    Bent in a swift and daring dream,
An ecstasy of trembling bliss,
And sealed together in a kiss,—
And the night waiting passion-spent.

Lovers.

FANTASIA.

WE 're all alone ! we 're all alone !
    The moon and stars are dead and gone,
The night 's at deep, the wind asleep,
And thou and I are all alone.

What care have we though life there be ?
Tumult and life are not for me !
Silence and sleep about us creep,
Tumult and life are not for thee !

How late it is since such as this
Had topped the height of breathing bliss !
And now we keep an iron sleep,—
In that grave thou, and I in this !

THE PRICE.

I.

THE velvet gloss of the purple chair
    Deepened beneath her yellow hair ;
Idly she folded and fluttered her fan,
Nor deigned a glance at the haughty man.

Soft was the robe she wore that night,
Softly her jewels shed their light ;
In lace, like the hoar-frost, fine and thin,
Rested the curve of her soft round chin.

Rich was the shadow of the room,
And warm the shifting fire-light's bloom
That lofty wall and ceiling sheathed,
Heavy the perfumed air she breathed.

The panel picture, half descried,
Opened a summer country-side ;

The statues in the ruddy gleam
Seemed happy spirits lost in dream.

From a tripod's crystal vase
Full-blown blossoms filled the place
With their fragance and delight,
Floated out in day's despite.

Sumptuous sense of costly cheer
Pervaded the bright atmosphere,
As if charmed walls had shut it in
From all the dark night's gusty din.

II.

The sad old year went out with rain,
The new year tapped upon the pane—
Tapped in a whirl of frozen snow,
And shrouded all the earth below.

Chill, as it silvered her casement o'er,
The pitiless wind blew over the moor,
Into the great black night o'erhead
The wild white storm forever fled.

Bitter, she knew, the stinging sleet
Far away on the moor-side beat—
Beat on a hillock hidden there,
And heaped on a broken heart's despair.

She shivered as though one touched the dead,
That grave-mound lay on her hope like lead ;
Round her the light and the warmth of breath,
Round him the desolate dark of death.

Oh, if she lay in that silent tomb—
If she were wrapped in that rayless gloom—
If those dear arms but clasped her in
Out of the black night's storm and sin !

But here a creature bartered and sold,
Bound by the baseness of hard red gold,
Held by the master, whose gloating eyes
Hovered like hawks above their prize.

III.

He leaned his arm on the mantle there,
He looked at her with her shining hair,
With her drooping eyes and her rosy chin,
And the dimples for smiles to gather in.

His from the dainty foot's slight tip
Up to the crimson of the lip—
His from the halo of the hair
To the white hand's magic in the air.

But never his the tender thought,
Not his the sigh with yearning fraught,
The conscious blush that flits and flies,
The lingering of impassioned eyes.

All her bearing seemed to say :
" I am yours.   Bid me obey.
But the rebel in my soul
Spurns to answer your control ! "

Of women she the peerless flower
So scornfully defied his power ;
The smouldering anger burned his heart,
Then blazed and tore his lips apart.

IV.

" Madam," said he, " since you are mine,
Lift those eyes and let them shine,
Sometimes, when you hear me speak,
Let the smile impinge your cheek."

" When you bought me, Sir," said she,
" You bought and paid for simply me ;
No one bargained for my smile—
It was not thought of all the while."

Said he : " Owe you naught beside—
Home, nor peace, where still hours glide ?
Morn means sunshine, song, and dew—
Are not smiles a part of you ? "

" Once, indeed, perhaps they were,"
She replied.   " Now, should they stir,
Smiles would be with all their blooms,
Like the funeral lamps in tombs."

"Though one shut you dungeon-deep
In his heart, awake, asleep—
Though he claim of you no more
Than the beggar at the door—"

But the lightnings of her eyes
More than swift and low replies,
Whose music hid the word they said
Sharper than an arrow-head.

Hushed and told him all was loss,
All his wealth but gilded dross ;
Bars retain nor rubies buy
Love, whose light wings cleave the sky.

"Ah ! 't is well you stand away—
Fire and flint disturb my clay ;
Else, although I am a slave,
Every day I dig your grave."

"Cruel words !" he answered her,
"Kinder eternal silence were,
Am I before you so unclean—
Easy to put a world between ?"

"Nay," she said, "make no ado,
Be to me as I to you.
When I pass you mind no more
Than a shadow on the floor."

Ah ! how fair th' unruffled face !
How complete the weary grace !
How remote the quiet tone—
She that should be all his own !

" See," he said, " I cannot sue,
Never was I taught to woo,
Yet I love you, though you make
Heart and soul within me ache."

She lifted both her snowy arms,
Loaded with his golden charms.
" If you love me, Sir," said she,
" Take your chains and set me free ! "

HEREAFTER.

LOVE, when all these years are silent, van-
     ished quite and laid to rest,
When you and I are sleeping, folded into one
     another's breast,
     When no morrow is before us, and the long
       grass tosses o'er us,
And our grave remains forgotten, or by alien
     footsteps pressed—

Still that love of ours will linger, that great love
     enrich the earth.
Sunshine in the heavenly azure, breezes blow-
     ing joyous mirth ;

Fragrance fanning off from flowers, melody
    of summer showers,
Sparkle of the spicy wood-fires round the happy
    autumn hearth.

That 's our love. But you and I, dear—shall we
    linger with it yet,
Mingled in one dew-drop, tangled in one sun-
    beam's golden net,
  On the violet's purple bosom—I the sheen,
    but you the blossom—
Stream on sunset winds and be the haze with
    which some hill is wet?

Or, beloved—if ascending—when we have en-
    dowed the world
With the best bloom of our being, whither will
    our way be whirled,
  Through what vast and starry spaces, toward
    what awful holy places,
With a white light on our faces, spirit over
    spirit furled?

Only this our yearning answers—wheresoe'er
    the way defile,
Not a film shall part us through the æons of
    that mighty while.
  In the fair eternal weather, even as phantoms
    still together,
Floating, floating, one forever, in the light of
    God's great smile!

LOUISE CHANDLER MOULTON.

SO blithely rose the happy day
　　When you and I began to kiss,
The birds believed December May,
So blithely rose the happy day,
And blossoms bloomed along our way,
　　Though it was time for snow, I wis—
So blithely rose the happy day
　　When you and I began to kiss.

Triolet.

AT MIDNIGHT.

THE room is cold and dark to-night—
　　The fire is low ;
Why come you, you who love the light,
　　To mock me so ?

I pray you leave me now alone ;
　　You worked your will,
And turned my heart to frozen stone ;
　　Why haunt me still ?

I got me to this empty place ;
　　I shut the door ;
Yet through the dark I see your face
　　Just as of yore.

The old smile curves your lips to-night.
        Your deep eyes glow
With that old gleam that made them bright
        So long ago.

I listen ; do I hear your tone
        The silence thrill?
Why come you?   I am alone,
        Why vex me still?

What!   Would you that we re-embrace—
        We two once more?
Are these your tears that wet my face
        Just as before?

You 'et me seek some new delight,
        Yet your tears flow.
What sorrow brings you back to-night?
        Shall I not know?

I will not let you grieve alone—
        The night is chill—
Though love is dead and hope is flown
        Pity lives still.

How silent is the empty space !
        Dreamed I once more ?
Henceforth against your haunting face
        I bar the door.

PARTING.

'TIS you, not I, have chosen. Love, go free |
   No cry of mine shall stop you on your way.
I wept above the dead Past yesterday,
Let it lie now where all fair dead things be,
Beneath the waves of Time's all-whelming sea.
Forget it or remember—come what may—
The time is past when one could bid it stay ;
What boots it any more to you or me ?
It was my life—what matter—I am dead,
And if I seem to move or speak, or smile,
If some strange round of being still I tread,
And am not buried, for a little while,
Yet, look you, Love, I am not what I seem,
I died when died my faith in that dear dream.

SONG

FILL the swift days full, my dear
   Since life is fleet ;
Love, and hold love fast, my dear,
   He is so sweet—
Sweetest, dearest, fleetest comer,
Fledgling of the sudden summer.

Love, but not too well, my dear !
   When skies are gray,

And the autumn winds are here,
  Love will away—
Fleetest, vaguest, farthest rover,
When the summer's warmth is over.

IF LOVE COULD LAST.

IF love could last, I 'd spend my all
  And think the price was yet too small
To buy his light upon my way,
His cheer whatever might befall.

Were I his slave, or he my thrall,
No terrors could my heart appall;
  I 'd fear no wreckage or dismay,
        If love could last.

Heaven's lilies grow up white and tall,
But warm within earth's garden wall—
  With roses red the soft winds play—
  Ah, might I gather them to-day !
My hands should never let them fall,
        If love *could* last !

NOW AND THEN.

AND had you loved me then, my dear,
  And had you loved me there,
When still the sun was in the east,
  And hope was in the air,—

When all the birds sang, in the dawn,
  And I but sang to you,—
And had you loved me then, my dear,
  And had you then been true !

But oh ! The day wore on, my dear,
  And when the noon grew hot,
The drowsy bird forgot to sing,
  And you and I
To talk of love, or live for faith,
  Or build ourselves a nest.
And now our hearts are shelterless,
  Our sun is in the west.

JOHN JAMES PIATT.

WHEN our half kisses meet, love,
  What marvels have birth !—
All fair things, and sweet, love,
  New Heaven, new Earth !

Counterparts.

HALF-LIVES.

TWO were they, two ; but one
  They might have been. Each knew
The other's spirit—fittest mate—apart.

Ah, hapless ! though once jealous Fortune drew
  Them almost heart to heart,
  In a brief-lighted sun !

So near they came, and then—they are so far !
  They seemed like two who pass,
Each on a world-long journey opposite,
  Their two trains hurrying dark
With long-drawn roar through the dread deep
      of night,
(O faces close—they almost touched, alas !
O hands that might have thrilled with meeting
      spark !
  O lips that might have kissed !
  O eyes with folded sight
  Dreaming some vision bright !)
  In darkness and in mist.

A ROSE'S JOURNEY.

HASTE on your gentle journey, sent
    To sweetest goal flower ever went :
Ah me, that cannot follow close—
But my heart runs before you, rose !

O happy rose, I envy you—
But sweetness makes such sweet grace due :
First to her lips one moment pressed,
Then your long heaven on her dear breast !

SALLIE M. B. PIATT.

WHISPER me, love, all things that are not
    true !

Life and Death.

TWELVE HOURS APART.

HE loved me.   But he loved, likewise,
  This morning's world in bloom and wings ;
Ah, does he love the world that lies
  In dampness, whispering shadowy things,
    Under this little band of noon ?

He loves me.   Will he fail to see
  A phantom hand has touched my hair,
(And wavered, withering, over me)
  To leave a subtle grayness there,
    Below the outer shine of June?

He loves me.   Would he call it fair,
  The flushed half-flower he left me, say ?
For it has passed beneath the glare
  And from my bosom drops away,
    Shaken into the grass with pain ?

He loves me ? Well, I do not know,
  A song in plumage crossed the hill

At sunrise when I felt him go—
  And song and plumage now are still,
    He could not praise the bird again.

He loves me? Veiled in mist I stand,
  My veins less high with life than when
To-day's thin dew was in the land,
  Vaguely less beautiful than then—
    Myself a dimness with the dim.

He loves me? I am faint with fear,
  He never saw me quite so old;
I never met him quite so near
  My grave, nor quite so pale and cold,
    —Nor quite so sweet, he says, to him!

IN DOUBT.

THROUGH dream and dusk a frightened
    whisper said:
"Lay down the world; the one you love is
    dead."
  In the near waters, without any cry,
  I sank, therefore—glad, oh, so glad, to die!

Far on the shore, with sun, and dove, and dew,
And apple-flowers, I suddenly saw you.
  Then—was it kind or cruel that the sea,
  Held back my hands, and kissed and clung
    to me?

8

WILLIAM WINTER.

I WILL drink to the woman who wrought my
    woe,
In the diamond morning of Long Ago.

Orgia.

REFUGE.

SET your face to the sea, fond lover,—
    Cold in darkness the sea-winds blow !
Waves and clouds and the night will cover
    All your passion and all your woe.
Sobbing waves and the death that is in them,
    Sweet as the lips that once you prest—
Pray that your hopeless heart may win them,
    Pray that your weary life may rest !

Set your face to the stars, fond lover,—
    Calm and silent, and bright and true,
They will pity you, they will hover
    Tenderly over the deep for you.
Winds of heaven will sigh your dirges,
    Tears of heaven for you be spent,
And sweet for you, will the murmuring surges
    Pour the wail of their low lament.

WITHERED ROSES.

NOT waked by worth, nor marred by flaw,
  Not won by good, nor lost by ill,
Love is its own and only law,
  And lives and dies by its own will.
It was our fate, and not our sin,
That we should love and love should win.

Not bound by oath, nor stayed by prayer,
  Nor held by thirst of strong desire,
Love lives like fragrance in the air,
  And dies as breaking waves expire.
'T was death, not falsehood, bade us part,—
The death of love that broke my heart.

Not kind, as dreaming poets think,
  Nor merciful, as sages say,—
Love heeds not where its victims sink,
  When once its heart is torn away.
'T was nature, it was not disdain,
That made thee careless of my pain.

Not thralled by law, nor ruled by right,
  Love keeps no audit with the skies:
Its star, that once is quenched in night,
  Has set,—and never more will rise.
My soul is dead, by thee forgot,
And there 's no heaven where thou art not.

But happy he, though scathed and lone,
  Who sees afar, love's fading wings,—
Whose seared and blighted soul has known
  The splendid agony it brings !
No life that is, no life to be,
Can ever take the past from me !

Red roses, bloom for other lives—
  Your withered leaves alone are mine !
Yet, not for all that time survives
  Would I your heavenly gift resign,—
Now cold and dead, once warm and true,
The love that lived and died in you.

WILLIAM DEAN HOWELLS.

O DARLING, and darling, and darling,
    If I dared to trust my thought ;
If I dared to believe what I must not,
    Believe what no one ought.

The Doubt.

FROM "NO LOVE LOST."

SOMETIMES, it seems that this love, which
   I feel is eternal,
Must have begun with my life, and that only an
   absence was ended

When we met and knew in our souls that we
    loved one another,
For from the first was no doubt. The earliest
    hints of the passion
Whispered to girlhood's tremulous dream, may
    be mixed with misgiving,
But, when very love comes, it bears no vague-
    ness of meaning.
Touched by its truth (too fine to be felt by the
    ignorant senses,
Knowing but looks and utterance), soul unto
    soul makes confession,
Silence to silence speaks. And I think that
    this subtile assurance
Yet unconfirmed from without, is even sweeter
    and dearer
Than the perfected bliss that comes when the
    words have been spoken.

THE THORN.

" EVERY Rose," you sang, " has its Thorn,
    But this has none, I know."
She clasped my rival's Rose
    Over her breast of snow.

I bowed to hide my pain,
    With a man's unskilful art,
I moved my lips, and could not say,
    The Thorn was in my heart.

CONVENTION.

HE falters on the threshold,
    She lingers on the stair;
Can it be that was his footstep?
    Can it be that she is there?

Without is tender yearning,
    And tender love is within;
They can hear each other's heart-beats,
    But a wooden door is between.

SARAH C. WOOLSEY.

"SUSAN COOLIDGE."

ROSES have thorns; and love is thorny, too;
    And this is love's sharp thorn which
      guards its flower,
   That our beloved have the cruel power
To hurt us deeper than all others do.

Thorns.

REPLY.

"WHAT, then, is Love?" she said.
    "Love is a music, blent in curious key,
Of jarring discords and of harmony;

'T is a delicious draught which, as you sip,
Turns sometimes into poison on your lip.
It is a sunny sky infolding storm,
The fire to ruin or the fire to warm ;
A garland of fresh roses fair to sight,
Which then becomes a chain and fetters tight.
It is a half-heard secret told to two,
A life-long puzzle or a guiding clue,
The joy of joys, the deepest pain of pains,
All these love has been and will be again."

  " How may I know ? " she said.
" Thou mayst not know, for Love has conned
      the art
To blind the reason and befool the heart.
So subtle is he, not himself may guess
Whether he shall be more or shall be less ;
Wrapped in a veil of many-colored mists
He flits disguisèd wheresoe'er he lists,
And for the moment is the thing he seems,
The child of vagrant hope and fairy dreams ;
Sails like a rainbow bubble on the wind,
Now high, now low, before us or behind ;
And only when your fingers grasp the prize
Changes his form and swiftly vanishes."

  " Then best not love," she said.
" Dear child, there is no better and no best ;
Love comes not, bides not at thy slight behest.

As well might thy frail fingers seek to stay
The march of waves in yonder land-locked bay,
As stem the surging tide which ebbs and fills
'Mid human energies and human wills.
The moon leads on the strong resisting sea ;
And so the moon of love shall beckon thee,
And at her bidding thou wilt leap and rise,
And follow o'er strange seas, 'neath unknown
      skies,
Unquestioning, to dash, or soon, or late,
On sand or cruel crag, as is thy fate."

  "Then woe is me," she said.
"Weep not, there is a harder, sadder thing,
Never to know this sweetest suffering !
Never to see the sun, though suns may slay,
Or share the richer feast as others may,
Sooner the sealed and closely guarded wine
Shall seek again his purple clustered vine,
Sooner the attar be again the rose,
Than love unlearn the secret that it knows !
Abide thy fate, whether for good or ill ;
Fearlessly wait, and be thou certain still
Whether as foe disguised or friendly guest,
He comes, Love's coming is of all things best."

TWO WAYS TO LOVE.

*" Dans l'amour il y a toujours l'un qui baise
et l'autre qui tend la joue."*

I.

HE says he loves me well, and I
   Believe it ; in my hands to make
Or mar, his life lies utterly ;
Nor can I the strong plea deny
   Which claims my love for his love's sake.

He says there is no face so fair
   As mine ; when I draw near, his eyes
Light up ; each ripple of my hair
He loves ; the very cloak I wear
   He touches gently where it lies.

And roses, roses all the way
   Upon my path fall, strewed by him ;
His tenderness by night, by day,
Keeps constant watch, and heaps alway
   My cup of pleasure to the brim.

The other women in their spite
   Count me the happiest woman born,
To be so worshipped ; I delight
To flaunt this homage in the sight
   Of all, and pay them scorn for scorn.

I love him—or I think I do :
   Sure one *must* love what is so sweet.
He is so tender and so true,
So eloquent to plead and sue,
   So strong, though kneeling at my feet.

Yet I had visions once of yore,
   Girlish imaginings of a zest,
A possible thrill,—but why run o'er
These fancies, idle dreams, no more.
   I will forget them, this is best.

So let him take—the past is past ;
   The future with its golden key
Into his outstretched hands I cast ;
I shall love him,—perhaps,—at last.
   As now I love his love for me.

II.

Not as all other women may,
   Love I my Love ; he is so great,
So beautiful, I dare essay
No nearness, but in silence lay
   My heart upon his path,—and wait.

Poor heart, its beatings are so low
   He does not heed them passing by,
Save as one heeds where violets grow
A fragrance, caring not to know
   Where the veiled purple buds may lie.

I sometimes think that it is dead,
  It lies so still.   I bend and lean
Like mother over cradle-head,
Listening if still faint breaths are shed
  Like sighs the parted lips between.

And then with vivid pulse and thrill
  It quickens into sudden bliss
At sound of step or voice, nor will
Be hushed, although, regardless still,
  He knows not, cares not, it is his.

I would not lift it if I could,
  The little flame, though faint and dim
As glowworm spark in lonely wood,
Shining where no man calls it good,
  May some day light the path for him.

May guide his way, or soon or late,
  Through blinding mist and falling rain,
And so content I watch and wait ;
Let others share his happier fate,
  I only ask to share his pain.

But if some day, when passing slow,
  My dear Love should his steps arrest,
Should spy the poor heart, bending low,
Should raise it, scan it, love it ?—so—
  Why,—God alone can tell the rest.

MARY MAPES DODGE.

THE leaping of heart unto heart with bliss
that can never be spoken.

Enfoldings.

SECRETS.

I 'D be like a daisy
　In the clover,
That I might look up bravely
　At my lover.

I 'd bid the willing breezes
　Bend me sweet,
That I might, as he passed me,
　Kiss his feet.

I 'd let the dew so quickly
　Start and glisten,
That, thinking I had called him,
　He would listen.

Yet would he listen vainly—
　Happy me !
No bee should find my secret,
　How could he ?

If ever the clover
 Couch he made,
I 'd softly kiss his eyelids
 In the shade.

Then would I breathe sweet incense
 All for him,
And fill with perfect bloom
 The twilight dim.

What should I do, I wonder,
 When he went?
Why I would—like a daisy—
 Be content.

Alack ! to live so bravely
 Peace o'erladen,
Has ne'er been granted yet
 To simple maiden.

READING.

ONE day in the bloom of a violet,
 I found a simple word ;
And my heart went softly humming it
 Till the violet must have heard.

And deep in the depths of a crimson rose
 A writing showed so plain,
I scanned it o'er in veriest joy
 To the patter of summer rain.

And then from the grateful mignonette
  I read—oh, such a thing!
That the glad tears fell on it like dew,
  And my soul was ready to sing.

A few little words ! Before that day
  I never had taken heed ;
But, oh, how I blessed the love that came—
  The love that taught me to read !

MARY CLEMMER AMES.

THERE is no distance,—not for those who
    know
The silent countersign that makes them one.
                              Distance.

GOOD-BY SWEETHEART.

GOOD-BY, Sweetheart!
    I leave thee with the loveliest things
The beauty-burdened spring-time brings—
The anemone in snowy hood,
The sweet arbutus in the wood ;
And to the smiling skies above
I say, " Bend lightly o'er my love " ;
And to the perfume-breathing breeze
I sigh, " Sing softest symphonies."
O lute-like leaves of laden trees,

Bear all your sweet refrain to him,
While in the June-time twilights dim
He thinks of me as I of him.
And so good-by, Sweetheart.

Good-by, Sweetheart !
I leave thee with the purest things,
That when some fair temptation sings
Its luring song, though sore beset,
Thou 'lt stronger be.   Then no regret
Life-long will follow after thee.
With touches lighter than the air
I kiss thy forehead brave and fair,
I say to God this last deep prayer :
" O guard him always, night and day,
So from thy peace he shall not stray."
And so good-by, Sweetheart.

Good-by, Sweetheart, we seem to part,
Yet still within my inmost heart
Thou goest with me.   Still my place
I hold in thine by love's dear grace ;
Yet all my life seems going out,
As slow I turn my face about,
To go alone till life's last day,
Unless thy smile can light my way—
Good-by, Sweetheart, the dreaded dawn
That tells our love's long tryst is gone
Is purpling all the pallid sky
As low I sigh, Sweetheart, good-by.

WORDS FOR PARTING.

OH, what shall I do, dear,
  In the coming years, I wonder,
When our paths, which lie so sweetly near,
  Shall lie so far asunder?
Oh, what shall I do, dear,
  Through all the sad to-morrows,
When the sunny smile has ceased to cheer,
  That smiles away my sorrows?

What shall I do, my friend,
  When you are gone forever?
My heart its eager need will send
  Through the years, to find you never.
And how will it be with you,
  In the weary world, I wonder,
Will you love me with a love as true
  When our paths lie far asunder?

A sweeter, sadder thing,
  My life for having known you,
Forever with its sacred kin,
  My soul's soul, I must own you,—
Forever mine, my friend,
  From June to life's December,—
Not mine to have or hold,
  But to pray for and remember.

JOHN HAY.

TO be deceived in your true heart's desire
    Is bitterer than a thousand years of fire.

A Woman's Love.

HOW IT HAPPENED.

I PRAY you, pardon me, Elsie,
    And smile that frown away
That dims the light of your lovely face
    As a thunder-cloud the day.
I really could not help it,—
    Before I thought 't was done,—
And those great gray eyes flashed bright and
        cold,
    Like icicles in the sun.

I was thinking of the summers
    When we were boys and girls,
And wandered in the blossoming woods,
    And the gay winds romped with your curls.
And you seemed to me the same little girl
    I kissed in the alder-path,
I kissed the little girl's lips, and alas !
    I have roused a woman's wrath.

There is not so much to pardon,—
  For why were your lips so red?
The blonde hair fell in a shower of gold
  From the proud, provoking head.
And the beauty that flashed from the splendid
     eyes,
  And played round the tender mouth,
Rushed over my soul like a warm sweet wind
  That blows from the fragrant south.

And where, after all, is the harm done?
  I believe we were made to be gay,
And all of youth not given to love
  Is vainly squandered away.
And strewn through life's low labors,
  Like gold in the desert sands,
Are love's sweet kisses and sighs and vows
  And the clasp of clinging hands.

And when you are old and lonely
  In Memory's magic shine,
You will see on your thin and wasting hands,—
  Like gems, these kisses of mine;
And when you muse at evening
  At the sound of some vanished name,
The ghost of my kisses shall touch your lips
  And kindle your heart to flame.

REMORSE.

SAD is the light of sunniest days
  Of love and rapture perished,
And shine through memory's tearful haze,
  The eyes once fondliest cherished.
Reproachful is the ghost of toys
  That charmed while life was wasted,
But saddest is the thought of joys
  That never yet were tasted.

Sad is the vague and tender dream
  Of dead love's lingering kisses,
To crushed hearts haloed by the gleam
  Of unreturning blisses,
Deep mourns the soul in anguished pride
  For the pitiless death that won them,—
But the saddest wail is for lips that died
  With the virgin dew upon them.

LAURA C. REDDEN.

"HOWARD GLYNDON."

THE sun stole to a red rose, and wiled her
    leaves apart,
May dew and June air had wooed her at the
    start,
But was 't not fair the sun should have her gol-
    den perfect heart?   *A Madrigal.*

DISARMED.

O LOVE, so sweet at first,
   So bitter in the end !
Thou canst be fiercest foe
   As well as fairest friend.
Are these poor withered leaves
   The fruitage of thy May ?
Thou that wert strong to save,
   How swift thou art to slay.

Ay, thou art swift to slay,
   Despite thy kiss and clasp,
Thy long, caressing look,
   Thy subtle, thrilling grasp !
Ay, swifter far to slay
   Than thou art strong to save,
And selfish in thy need,
   And cruel as the grave.

Yes, cruel as the grave.
   Go, go, and come no more !
But canst thou set my heart
   Just where it was before ?
Go, go, and come no more !
   Go, leave me with thy tears,
The only gift of thine
   That shall outlive the years.

Yet shall outlive the years
　One other cherished thing,
Light as a vagrant plume
　Shed from some passing wing :—
The memory of thy first
　Divine, half-timid kiss,
Go ! I forgive thee all
　In weeping over this !

QUITS.

I AM the victor, Philip May !
　You knew it the moment we met to-night.
You had not looked for such easy grace,
　For our parting left me crushed and white.
My lips were curved in a quiet smile—
　You had seen them stiffen with sudden pain—
Did you think as you searched my eyes the
　　　while,
　Of the times they had looked for you in vain ?

Did they tell you the story you hoped to read ?
　—The tale of a lingering love for you ?—
Why did you quail and falter so,
　'Neath the level ray of their frozen blue ?
Why did you drop your faultless voice
　To the tender tone of the olden strain ?
—You cannot recall the early trust
　Whose delicate life by scorn was slain !

You 're foiled for once, my king of hearts!
  Mine was too high to break for you.
I might have loved you long and well,
  Had I proved you noble and good and true.
But when I saw that the thing I loved
  Was not you, but my soul's Ideal,—
When I knew you selfish and hard and cold,—
  I had no fealty for the Real.

You are not my master any more!
  Your thrall of the olden time is free,
The broken wing of the bird is healed,
  And I scorn your pliant tongue and knee.
Have you forgotten your spoken words?
  I shall remember them till I die ;—
My heart went down in the dust to you,
  And low in the dust you let it lie !

You have mistaken me all the while,
  I do not miss you, nor want you now !
The lesson you taught me is potent yet,
  Though it left no line on my open brow.
Clever player, of cunning touch,
  The chords are jangled and will not chime !
Well, are the throes of a tortured heart
  Set to the flow of a pleasant rhyme ?

But God, he knows that I had no hope
  Ever to lure you back again ;

And the wish went out with the Long Ago,
  And never can come to me again.
How dared you dream you were dear to me?
  Or speak of things that you should forget?
I blush to think a kiss of yours
  Ever upon my mouth was set !

The love that I bore you, Philip May,
  Nearly killed me ere it died ;
But one dark night the stubborn thing
  Was sternly stifled and pushed aside.
And the arms of a true love took in me,
  Whom you left to moan at your heart's shut
        door ;
I 'm clothed about with his tenderness,
  And wrapped from loneness evermore !

JOAQUIN MILLER.

BETTER sit still where born, I say,
  Wed one sweet woman and love her well,
Love and be loved in the old East way,
  Drink sweet waters and dream in a spell,
Than to wander in search of the Blessed Isles,
And to sail the thousands of watery miles
In the search of love, and find you at last
On the edge of the world, and a cursed outcast.

Pace Implora.

STANZAS FROM "THE IDEAL AND THE REAL."

WE two had been parted—God pity us !—
    when
The stars were unnamed and all heaven was
    dim ;
We two had been parted far back on the rim
And the outermost border of heaven's red bars ;
We two had been parted ere the meeting of men,
Or God had set compass on spaces as yet.
We two had been parted ere God had set
His finger to spinning the purple with stars,—
And now, at the last in the gold and set
Of the sun in Venice, we two had met.

   *   *   *   *   *   *

I saw her one moment, then fell back abashed,
And filled full to the throat—then I turned me
    once more
So glad to the sea, while the level sun flashed
On the far snowy Alps—her breast !—why, her
    breast
Was white as twin pillows that lure you to rest,
Her sloping limbs moved like to melodies, told
As she rose from the sea, and she threw back
    the gold
Of her glorious hair, and set face to the shore.—
I knew her, I knew her, though we had not met
Since the far stars sang to the sun's first set.

How long I had sought her !   I had hungered
    nor ate
Of my sweet fruits, I had tasted not one
Of all the fair glories under the sun.
I had sought only her.   Yea, I knew that she
Had come upon earth, and stood waiting for me
Somewhere by my way.   But the pathways of
    fate
They had led otherwhere, the round world
    round.
The far North seas and the near profound
Had failed me for aye.   Now I stood by that sea
Where ships drave in, and all dreamily.

    *   *   *   *   *   *

I spake not, but caught at my breath, I did
    raise
My face to fair heaven, to give God praise
That at last, ere the ending of time, we two
Had touched upon earth at the same sweet
    place—
Never, since ages ere Adam's fall
Had we two met in fulness of soul,
Where two are as one, but had wandered on
    through
The spheres divided, where planets roll
Unnamed and in darkness through limitless
    space.

RECOLLECTION.

SOME things are sooner marred than made,
   The moon was white, the stars a-chill—
A frost fell on a soul that night,
And lips were whiter, colder still.
A soul was black that erst was white,
And you forget the place—the night !
Forget that aught was done or said—
Say this has passed a long decade—
Say not a single tear was shed—
Say you forget these little things !
Is not your recollection loath ?
Well, little bees have little stings,
And I remember for us both.

SONG.

THERE is many a love in the land, my love,
   But never a love like this is ;
Then kill me dead with your love, my love,
   And cover me up with kisses.

So kill me dead and cover me deep
   Where never a soul discovers ;
Deep in your heart to sleep, to sleep,
   In the darlingest tomb of lovers.

A FAREWELL.

FAREWELL, farewell! for aye, farewell.
  Yet must I end as I began.
I love you, love you, love but you—
I love you now as never man
Has loved since man and woman fell,
Or God gave man inheritance,
Or sense of love, or any sense.
And that is why, O Love, I can
Lift up to you my burning brow
To-night, and so renounce you now.

TO FLORENCE.

IF all God's world a garden were,
  If women were but flowers ;
If men were bees that busied there,
  Through all the summer hours,—
Oh, I would hum God's garden through
For honey, till I came to you.

Then I should hive within your hair,
  Its sun and gold together :
And I should hide in glory there,
  Through all the changeful weather.
Oh ! I should sip but one, this one
Sweet flower beneath the sun.

Oh, I would be a king, and coin
Your golden hair in money;
And I would only have to seek
Your lips for hoards of honey.
Oh! I would be the richest king
That ever wore a signet-ring.

NORA PERRY.

TYING her bonnet under her chin,
She tied her raven ringlets in,
But not alone in the silken snare
Did she catch her lovely floating hair,
For, tying her bonnet under her chin,
She tied a young man's heart within.

The Love-Knot.

THE KING'S KISS.

"HOW long," he asked, "will you remember
this—
How long?" Then downward bent
His kingly head, and on her lips a kiss
Fell like a flame—a flame that sent
Through every vein
Love's joy and pain;
"How long," he asked, "will you remember
this?"

"How long?" she lifted from his breast a
        cheek
    Red with her sacred love,
Yet when her redder lips essayed to speak,
    And when her heart did move
            To answer grave and sweet,
            Somehow a smile unmeet
Broke waywardly across red lips and cheek.

"How long, how long will I remember this?
    Say *you*," she murmured low—
"Say you"—and while she trembled with her
        bliss,
    That smile went to and fro
            Across her flushing face,
            And hid a graver grace—
"Say you, how long will you remember this?"

He bent above her in that moment's bliss,
    He held her close and fast :
"How long, how long will I remember this?
    Until I cross at last,
            With failing, dying breath,
            That river men call Death—
So long, so long, will I remember this!"

But, when apart they stood, did he remember
    His words that summer day?
Did he remember through the long December
    The warmth and love of May,

The warmth, and love, and bliss,
The meaning of that kiss,
When kingdoms stood between—did he re-
member?

Ah ! who can say for him ?   For her we know
The king's kiss was her crown ;
For her we know no agony of woe,
No other smile or frown,
Could make her heart forswear
That summer morning there,
Beneath the forest-trees of Fontainebleau.

RIDING DOWN.

OH, did you see him riding down
And riding down, while all the town
Came out to see, came out to see,
And all the bells rang mad with glee ?

Oh, did you hear those bells ring out,
The bells ring out, the people shout ;
And did you hear that cheer on cheer
That over all the bells rang clear ?

And did you see the waving flags,
The fluttering flags, the tattered rags,
Red, white, and blue, shot through and through,
Baptized with battle's deadly dew ?

And did you hear the drums' gay beat,
The drums' gay beat, the music sweet,
The cymbals' clash, the cannons' crash,
That rent the sky with sound and flash?

And did you see me waiting there,
And waiting there, and watching there,
One little lass, amid the mass
That pressed to see the hero pass?

And did you see him smiling down,
And smiling down, as riding down
With slowest pace, with stately grace,
He caught the vision of a face,—

My face uplifted red and white,
Turned red and white with sheer delight,
To meet the eyes, the smiling eyes,
Outflashing in their swift surprise?

Oh, did you see how swift it came,
How swift it came, like sudden flame,
That smile to me, to only me,
The little lass who blushed to see?

And at the windows all along,
Oh, all along, a lovely throng
Of faces fair, beyond compare,
Beamed out upon him riding there!

Each face was like a radiant gem,
A sparkling gem, and yet for them
No swift smile came, like sudden flame,
No arrowy glance took certain aim.

He turned away from all their grace,
From all that grace of perfect face,
He turned to me, to only me,
The little lass who blushed to see !

SIDNEY LANIER.

So one in heart and thought, I trow
  That thou mightst press the strings and I
    might draw the bow,
And both would meet in music sweet,
    Thou and I, I trow.
        Thou and I.

IN ABSENCE.

The storm that snapped our fate's one ship in
    twain
  Hath blown my half o' the wreck from thine
    apart.
O Love ! O Love ! across the gray-waved main
  To thee-ward strain my eyes, my arms, my
    heart.

I ask my God if e'en in His sweet place
  Where by one waving of a wistful wing
My soul could straightway tremble face to face
  With thee, with thee, across the stellar ring—
Yea, where thine absence I could ne'er bewail
  Longer than lasts that little blank of bliss
When lips draw back with recent pressure pale,
  To round and redden for another kiss—
    Would not my lonesome heart still sigh for
      thee
    What time the drear kiss intervals must be?

So do the mottled formulas of Sense
  Glide snake-wise through our dreams **of**
    Aftertime;
So errors breed in reeds and grasses dense
  That bank our singing rivulets of rhyme.
By Sense rule Space and Time; but in **God's**
    land
  Their intervals are not, save such as lie
Betwixt successive tones in concords bland
  Whose loving distance makes the harmony.
Ah, there shall never come 'twixt me and thee
  Gross dissonances of the mile, the year,
But in the multichords of ecstasy
  Our souls shall mingle, yet be featured clear,
    And absence wrought in intervals divine
    Shall part, yet link, thy nature's tone and
      mine.
      10

Look down the shining peaks of all my days,
  Base-hidden in the valleys of deep night,
So shalt thou see the heights and depths of
      praise
  My love would render unto love's delight ;
For I would make each day an Alp sublime
  Of passionate snow, white-hot yet icy-clear,
—One crystal of the true-loves of all time
  Spiring the world's prismatic atmosphere ;
And I would make each night an awful vale,
  Deep as thy soul, obscure as modesty,
With every star in heaven trembling pale
  O'er sweet profounds where only Love can see.
    Oh, runs not thus the lesson thou hast
      taught ?—
    Where life 's all love, 't is life : aught else,
      't is naught.

Let no man say, *He at his lady's feet*
  Lays worship that to Heaven alone belongs ;
Yea, sings the incense that for God is meet
  In flippant censers of light lovers' songs.
Who says it, knows not God, nor love, nor thee ;
  For love is large as is yon heavenly dome :
In love's great blue each passion is full free
  To fly his favorite flight and build his home.
Did e'er a lark with skyward pointing beak
  Stab by mischance a level-flying dove ?
Wife-love flies level, his dear mate to seek :

God-love darts straight into the skies above.
  Crossing the windage of each other's wings,
  But speeds **them both upon their jour-**
    neyings.

EVENING SONG.

L OOK off, dear love, across the sallow sands,
  And mark **you** meeting of the sun and sea,
How long they kiss in sight of all the lands.
  Ah ! longer, love, kiss we.

Now in the sea's red vintage melts the sun,
  As Egypt's pearl dissolved in rosy wine,
And Cleopatra-night, drinks all. 'T is done,
  Love, lay thine hand in mine.

Come forth, sweet stars, and comfort heaven's
    heart ;
  Glimmer, ye waves, round else unlighted
    sands,
O night ! divorce our sun and sky apart,
  Never our lips, our hands.

THOMAS S. COLLIER.

YOU ask what love is.   It is this, my own,
  To hold all women pure because **of you**,
Yet give heart-reverence unto *you* alone,
  And for your sake be steadfast, brave, **and**
    true.

Love.

CLEOPATRA DYING.

SINKS the sun below the desert,
  Golden glows the sluggish Nile ;
Purple flame crowns sphinx and temple,
  Lights up every ancient pile
Where the old gods now are sleeping ;
  Isis and Osiris great,
Guard me, help me, give me courage
  Like a queen to meet my fate !

"**I am** dying, Egypt, dying !"
  Let the Cæsar's army come—
I will cheat him of his glory,
  Though beyond the Styx I roam.
Shall he drag this beauty with him
  While **the** crowd his triumph **sings ?**
No, no, never !   I will show him
  What lies in the blood of kings.

Though he hold the golden sceptre,
  Rule the Pharaoh's sunny land,
Where old Nilus rolls resistless,
  Through the sweeps of silvery sand,
He shall never say I met him
  Fawning, abject, like a slave—
I will foil him, though **to** do **it**
  I must cross the Stygian wave.

Oh, my hero, sleeping, sleeping—
  Shall I meet you on the shore
Of Plutonian shadows? Shall we
  In death meet and love once more?
See, I follow **in your** footsteps—
  Scorn the Cæsar and his might;
For your love I will leap boldly
  Into realms of death and night.

Down below the desert sinking,
  Fades Apollo's brilliant car,
And from out the distant azure
  Breaks the bright gleam of a star;
Venus, queen of love and beauty,
  Welcomes me to death's embrace,
Dying free, proud, and triumphant,
  The last sovereign of my race.

Dying! dying! **I am coming,**
  Oh, my hero, to your arms!

You will welcome me, I know it—
  Guard me from all rude alarms.
Hark ! I hear the legions coming,
  Hear their cries of triumph swell,
But, proud Cæsar, dead I scorn you,
  Egypt—Antony—farewell !

IN LOVE'S DEFENSE.

WHEN love like a red rose burns and blushes,
  How sweet is the kiss that warm lips give ;
The soul's far deep at its coming hushes
  The thirsting passions that in them live.

And fair as a lily, newly breaking
  The odorous sleep of its natal gloom,
Is the pure, white flame, to glory waking,
  As fragrant blossoms unfold in bloom.

Oh, Love that fills us with visions tender,
  What gift can we give befitting thee ?
What gem can the mines unto thee render ?
  What pearl from caves in the lustrous sea ?

With hands that tremble, and steps that falter,
  We bring our gold, or our dross, and claim
A draught of fire from the radiant altar,
  And win our tithe of the sacred flame.

It may be sweet, or it may be bitter,
  But thou, dear Love, hast no blame for this ;
Not thine are the eyes that falsely glitter,
  Not thine are the lips that falsely kiss.

For one man wins from another's labor,
  The heavy grain of the harvest home ;
And by the blows of his foeman's sabre,
  The rightful prince to his throne shall come.

And thou, when we ask the gift most fitting,
  Will unto our needs be true and just ;
It is we who break the thread in the knitting,
  And pluck the fruit that is made of dust.

It is ours, the blow whose dissonance clashes,
  Through valleys loud with the ringing song ;
If we shun thy flame for fireless ashes,
  And our hearts grow cold, we do thee wrong.

For fair, as when first thy dart went speeding
  Through glooms made bright by the violet's
      breath,
Are thy gifts, if our souls were not unheeding,
  And would not quaff what will bring thee
      death.

The vanished years, and the years before us,
  Can win from thy lips no song sublime,
That does not echo amid the chorus,
  Thrilling our souls in the present time.

DAVID L. PROUDFIT.
"PELEG ARKWRIGHT."

" IT 's hard ! I might have knowed it !
  It seems to be the rule,
Where women hold the ribbons
  For men to play the fool.
There must have been some contract
  Delivered, sealed, and signed,
To give the power to females
  To crucify mankind."

Love in a Shop.

LOVE IN OYSTER BAY.

I AIN'T anybody in particular,
  And never calc'lated to be ;
I 'm aware that my views does n't signify
  Except to Belinda and me,
But I 'm heavy on openin' oysters—
  In regards to them I am free
To remark, that fur shellin' of Blue Points,
  There is few that can lay over me.

Excuse my perfessional blowin'—
  It is n't the point I would make ;
But I 'm feelin' particular airy
  An' uncommonly wide-awake ;

An' I 've got to be talkin' about it—
  It won't lay quiet y' see,—
Which the name of the girl is Belinda
  That 's took an affection for me.

It 's surprisin'! The fact is surprisin'!
  Just cast your eye over this frame—
Is there any thing specially gallus,
  Which characterizes the same?
As a model fur makin' wax-figgers
  I should n't make much of a stir;
But I ain't a-goin' to worry
  So long as I 'm pleasin' to her.

An impediment hinders my speakin'
  As I should admire to do ;
As an elocution professor
  My scholars would likely be few ;
But she said when I mentioned it to her,
  " Why, dear, don 't you fret, for you see,
You tell me you love me, my darling,
  And your voice is like music to me."

I was never indicted for intellect,
  Nor never arrested for cheek,
But I 'm holdin' my head elevated
  Since Thursday night was a week,
Fur that was the date when Belinda
  Allowed she was partial to me,

And give me a relish fur livin'
  An' a notion of workin' fur she.

She is n't egzackly a beauty,
  And also she uses a crutch;
But the eyes of that dear little cripple
  The heart of an oyster would touch;
They is wonderful soft, and so lovin'—
  A good-lookin' face on the whole,
Fur the light in them eyes seems to travel
  Right out from a beautiful soul.

If she had been lively and hearty
  I could n't have helped her, y' see;
An' similar then, it ain't likely
  That she would have took up with me.
An' I would n't uv knowed her and loved her,
  So patient and gentle and sweet;
An' I wish that the whole of creation
  I could lay at her poor little feet.

I was never so chirk an' galloptious,
  An' never before felt so spry,
An' I 've just took to noticin' lately
  How amazin'ly blue is the sky;
An' how gay is the stars in the night-time,
  A-winkin' an' glimmerin' down—
Good gracious! I come near forgettin'
  That barrel of oysters for Brown.

A KISS.

AH, rosebud mouth, for kisses made,
   And you **are** not the least afraid?
And do not know, my little **one**,
What mischief kisses sweet have done?
O'er all the world and through all time,
In every age and every clime,
Men have kissed women's mouths, and still,
Through every coming age they will,
While rolls the world the ether through,
What then? **That** should I not tell **you.**

I love you, darling, but I know
What way the summer zephyrs blow.
And you love me, but in your heart
Love sitteth, pensive and apart
Demure, serene, and lost in dreams
Of all that is and all that seems.
You know not even why it is
That you are startled by a kiss.

But I, a veteran, scarred and worn,
On battle surges tossed and torn,
And scorched by passion's fiery breath;
I that have been playmate with death,
And mocked the heavy hand of fate,
And plumbed the depths of love and hate,

I know, my little star-eyed miss,
Why devils laugh when mortals kiss.

Alas, and who shall count the cost
Of human souls for love's sake lost?
For peasant's hut, and kingly crown,
And rural dell, and stately town,
And vineyards ripening in the sun,
And kingdoms by the strong arm won,
And armies marshalled for the fray,
Have been o'erthrown and swept away,
Betrayed and wrecked and lost for this,
The needless harvest of **a** kiss.

Nathless, but there is loss and gain,
And oft a kiss has banished pain,
And dowered the world with splendid light
And flushed the day with beauty bright,
And bade the earth and sea and sky,
Take rapturous heed that heaven is nigh;
And since the first sad soul was lost
Not one has stopped to count the cost.

What then? What then? I kiss you, dear,
And **kiss** away that trembling tear.
What need for me to say, my sweet,
What serpents sting unwary feet?
If storms are gathering, let them break;
Yea, if the starry heavens quake,

And suns are quenched, and if the **world**
To crashing ruin should be hurled,
On verge of vast eternity
I'd kiss you, kiss you, what care we?

EXTRACT FROM "LOVE IN A KITCHEN."

"WELL, thin, will it plaze ye to give **me**
the kiss?"
"Git out wid yer blarney! shure how can **I**
tell
But there might be another would suit me as
well?"
"Arrah, Kitty, me darlin', don't say that agin,
If ye wouldn't be killin' the thruest of min;
But if there's another ye like more than me,
Thin its faithless ye are, and it's goin' I'll be,
An' I'll die broken-hearted fur lack of the joy
That I thought to be gainin'——"

                          "Why, Teddy, me boy,
Is it dyin' ye 'r shpakin' of? What would I do;
An' unmarried widda in mournin' for you?
An' ye wanted a kiss? Well, there, if ye must—
Oh, murther, the man is devourin' me just!
Is it atin' me ye'd be afther, belike?
Well, it's not so ouplazin', ye may, if ye like;
An' if any one's askin' about ye, I'll own
That a broth of a boy is me Teddy Malone!"

RICHARD WATSON GILDER.

YOU may sound the sources of life,
    And prate of its aim and scope ;
You may search with your chilly knife
    Through the broken heart of hope.
But for me the love-sweet breath,
    And the warm, white bosom heaving,
And never a thought of death,
    And only the bliss of living.

The Poet's Protest.

THE DARK ROOM.

A PARABLE.

I.

A MAIDEN sought her love in a dark room,—
    So early had she yearned from yearning
      sleep,
    So hard it was from her true love to keep,—
    And blind she went through that all-silent
      gloom,
Like one who wanders weeping in a tomb.
    Heavy her heart, but her light fingers leap
    With restless grasp and question in that deep
    Unanswering void. Now when a hand did
      loom

At last, how swift her warm impassioned face
  Pressed 'gainst the black and solemn-yielding
    air,
  As near, more near, she groped to that bright
    place,
And seized the hand, and drowned it with her
    hair,
  And bent her body to his fierce embrace,
  And knew what joy was in the darkness there.

II.

Great God! the arms wherein that maiden fell
  Were not her lover's; I am her lover—I,
  Who sat here in the shadows silently—
  Silent with gladness, for I thought, O hell!
I thought to me she moved, and all was well.
  She saw me not, yet dimly could descry
  That beautiful hand of his, and with a sigh
  Sank on his fair and treacherous breast. The
    spell
Of the Evil One was on me. All in vain
  I strove to speak—my parchèd lips were
    dumb.
  See! see! the wan and whitening window-
    pane!
See, in the night, the awful morning bloom!
  Too late she will know all! Heaven! send
    thy rain
  Of death, nor let the sun of waking come!

I COUNT MY TIME BY TIMES THAT I MEET THEE.

I COUNT my time by times that I meet thee;
  These are my yesterdays, my morrows,
      noons,
  And nights.   These my old moons and my
      new moons.
  Slow fly the hours, or fast the hours do flee,
If thou art far from or art near to me:
  If thou art far, the birds' tunes are no tunes;
  If thou art near, the wintry days are Junes,—
  Darkness is light, and sorrow cannot be.
Thou art my dream come true, and thou my
      dream,
  The air I breathe, the world wherein I dwell;
  My journey's end thou art, and thou the
      way;
Thou art what I would be, yet only seem;
  Thou art my heaven and thou art my hell;
  Thou art my ever-living judgment day.

MY SONGS ARE ALL OF THEE.

MY songs are all of thee, what though I sing
    Of morning, when the stars are yet in
      sight,
  Of evening, or the melancholy night,
  Of birds that o'er the reddening waters wing;

Of song, of fire, of winds, or mists that cling
  To mountain tops, of winter all in white,
  Of rivers that toward ocean take their flight,
  Of summer, when the rose is blossoming.
I think no thought that is not thine, no breath
  Of life I breathe beyond thy sanctity ;
  Thou art the voice that silence uttereth.
And of all sound thou art the sense.   From thee
  The music of my song, and what it saith
  Is but the beat of thy heart, throbbed through
      me.

ELIZABETH STUART-PHELPS-WARD.

AH ! who can sing of any thing,
    With none to listen lovingly ?
                    Broken Rhythm.

WHAT THE VIOLINS SAID.

SONG.

"' We 're all for love,' the violins said."
                    SIDNEY LANIER.

DO I love you ?   Do I love you ?
    Ask the heavens that bend above you
To find language and to prove you
    If they love the living sun.

11

Ask the burning, blinded meadows
If they love the falling shadows,
If they hold the happy shadows
  When the fervid day is **done.**

Ask the blue-bells and the daisies,
Lost amid the hot field-mazes,
Lifting up their thirsty faces,
  If they love the summer rains.
Ask the linnets and the plovers,
In the nest-life made for lovers,
Ask the bees and ask the clovers—
  Will they tell you for your pains?

Do I, Darling, do I love you?
What, I pray, can that behoove you?
How in Love's name can I move you?
  When for Love's sake I am dumb?
If I told you, if I told you,
Would that keep you, would that hold you,
Here at last where I enfold you?
  If **it** would—hush! Darling, come!

TOLD IN CONFIDENCE.

VOW you 'll never, never tell him!
  Freezing stars now glittering farthest,
    fairest on the winter sky ;
If he woo me,

Not your coldest, cruel ray
    Or can or may
Be found more chill and still to him than I.

  Swear you 'll never, never tell him!
Warm, red roses lifting your shy faces to
            the summer dew;
    If he win me,
    Blush your sweetest in his sight
    For his delight,
But I can be as warm and sweet as you.

WILL CARLETON.

" WELL, so far as I can see,
    In the line of love an' lovin', what 's to
        be is apt to be."
                    The New Lochinvar.

ONE AND TWO.

IF you to me be cold,
    Or I be false to you,
The world will go on, I think,
Just as it used to do:
The clouds will flirt with the moon,
The sun will kiss the sea,

The wind to the trees will whisper,
And laugh at you and me.
But the sun will not shine so bright,
The clouds will not seem so white,
To one as they will to two ;
So I think you had better be kind,
And I had best be true,
And let the old love go on,
Just as it used to do.

If the whole of a page be read,
If a book be finished through,
Still the world may read on, I think,
Just as it used to do :
For other lovers will con
The pages we have passed,
And the treacherous gold of the binding
Will glitter unto the last.
But lids have a lonely look,
And one may not read the book
It opens only to two ;
So I think you had better be kind,
And I had best be true,
And let the reading go on,
Just as it used to do.

If we who have sailed together
Flit out of each other's view,
The world will sail on, **I** think,

Just as it used to do :
And we may reckon by stars
That flash from different skies,
And another of Love's pirates
May capture my lost prize.
But ships long time together
Can better the tempest weather
Than any other two ;
So I think you had better be kind,
And I had best be true,
That we together may sail,
Just as we used to do.

TWELVE O'CLOCK.

A LEGEND OF BROOKLYN.

"'DO I love you ? '   O but listen !"
          And he saw her dark eyes glisten
With a gentle joy that filled him,
With a passion wave that thrilled him.
"'Do I love you ? '   Ask the ages
Front of this life's blotted pages—
Cycles that our minds forget,
But our souls remember yet—
If the strands they saw us twine
In great moments half divine
Cannot stand against the cold
Voice and touch of senseless gold ?
How can wealth forbid the meeting

Of **two** hearts that blend in beating?
How can thrift presume to fashion
Heaven's eternal love and passion?
Listen! If 't is not o'er soon,
Come to-morrow-day at noon—
On that glad, that mournful day,
When my girlhood creeps away;
On that day—the understood
Birthday of my womanhood—
Come! and, joined in hand as heart,
We will walk no more apart.
Meet me—do not let me wait—
By this iron—this golden—gate
When, its mid-day hour to tell,
Rings the silvery Court-house bell.

"Should I fail you, dear, to-morrow,
Go away, but not in sorrow;
There be many ways may meet
Fetters round a maiden's feet.
There be watchers, there be spies,
There be jealous tongues and eyes;
Many hate my love for you,
And would cut our love in two.
Oh, they guard me all the time,
As if loving were a crime!

"Should I fail the second morrow,
Hope from next day you must borrow.

If I fail you then—endure;
Hope and trust be still the cure.
Naught on earth has power—has art—
Long to hold us two apart.
None but God were equal to it,
And I know He would not do it.
I will come to you, indeed.
You would wait, love, were there need?"
And he said, with brave endeavor:
" I will wait for you forever.
Each day I will come for **you,**
Till you come and find me true.
Each day hear the hopeful swell
Of the mid-day Court-house bell."

So next day he stood and waited
For the soul his soul had mated;
Saw the clock's black finger climb
To its topmost round of time;
Heard the mighty metal throat
Sing afar its mid-day note;
Listened with a nervous thrill
And his warm heart standing still;
Glanced about with keen desire
And his yearning soul afire;
Searched and searched with jealous care—
Searched, but saw no loved one there.
" ' Should I fail **you, love,** to-morrow,
Go away, but not in **sorrow,**'

'T was her word," he softly said.
" Be she living, be she dead,
Still my heart is scant of fear ;
She will some time meet me here.
My sad soul I will employ
With to-morrow's destined joy ;
Here is happiness for me,
Living o'er what is to be.
She will come—her love to tell—
With to-morrow's mid-day bell."

So next day he watched and waited
With a heart by hope elated ;
Peering—searching for a face
Full of love-exalted grace.
But his glance crept far and wide,
With some fear it could not hide ;
Crept across the grimy pavement,
Moaning in its dull enslavement ;
Roamed the long streets, empty seeming
Though with lovely faces gleaming ;
Shivered, as with landscape drear,
'Neath a blue sky bright and clear ;
For the bell, with sorrowing strain,
Called her to his side in vain.
" ' If I fail the second morrow,
Hope from next day you must borrow,'
'T was her word," he bravely said,
" Let to-morrow stand instead."

Still upon his heart there fell
Shadows from the mid-day bell.

Day by day he watched and waited,
By cold Disappointment **fated;**
Bit by bit his hoping ceased;
Hour by hour his faith increased.
Oft he strove to find her then,
In her guardian's palace den.
But the looks he met were bleak,
And the marble **would** not speak;
Would not show the poisoned thong
Of a dark and fiendish wrong;
Would not tell **the** woe and rage
Of a dreary mad-house cage,
Where the girl was kept by stealth,
Lest she claim her paltry wealth;
Could not hear her frantic prayer
That God's hand might reach her **there;**
Could not see her droop away,
Hour by hour and day by **day;**
Could not feel her breath grow still
With the healing arts that kill;
Could not trace the greed that gave
Her a half-named marble grave.
Still he watched and waited well
'Neath the weary noontide bell.

Days and weeks and months and years
Coursed the face **of** time like tears—

Spring's sweet-scented mid-day air,
Summer's fierce meridian glare,
Autumn's mingled lead and gold,
Winter's murder thrusts of cold.
Patiently he braved each one
At its mid-day cloud or sun ;
Silently he turned—was gone—
Sad, desponding, and alone.
Still his famished eyes crept round,
Still he thrilled at every sound.
" ' Naught on earth has power—has art—
Long to hold us two apart.
None but God were equal to it,
And I know He would not do it ; '
'T was her word," he grimly said ;
" She will come, alive or dead."
Pavement travellers passed him by
Day by day with curious eye ;
Dreamers sought romance to trace
In his bronzed and fading face ;
Questioners, though kind, were yet
With cold patient silence met ;
Still he watched and waited well
By the lonely Court-house bell.

Yet he came, yet crept away ;
And his dark brown hair grew gray,
And his manhood's power grew spent,
And his form grew thin and bent.

Poorly clad **and** rough to see,
Crushed by sickness' stern decree,
For intense compassion fit,
But still grandly scorning it.
" He is crazed," they said, aside.
"I am sane !" his heart replied.
" ' I will come to you, indeed ;
You would wait, love, were there need?'
'T was her word," he faintly said.
" Hands will meet if hearts are wed."
Sometimes to him it would seem—
Half in earnest, half in dream—
He could view her loveliness,
He could feel her fond caress.
But some passing sound or sight
Sent the vision back to night ;
And a dull and mournful knell
Seemed the leaden Court-house bell.

As one day his weakened form
Bent before a winter storm,
As he fell—Death's form before him
And a veil of darkness o'er him—
Soft a voice—or was it seeming ?—
Full a form—or was he dreaming ?—
Brought a rapture that repaid
All the debts that grief had made.
"Oh, my love !"—the words came fast—
" Do you see me, then, at last ?

Do you hear me ?   Do you feel me ?
Can the world no more conceal me ?
'Did I meet you ? '   Oh, but listen !
When released from pain's black prison,
Long through gardens and through meadows,
Long through death's black silent shadows,
With my soul God's help entreating,
Sought I for our place of meeting.

" Oh, I crushed my arms around you
When I found you—when I found you ;
Saw your sorrow's black net weaving ;
Fondly suffering, bravely grieving ;
Saw the truth you could not see ;
Felt your loving faith in me.
How each day—God's help entreating—
Came I to our place of meeting !
How I hailed each welcome morrow !
How I strove to soothe your sorrow !
Times the thought would come to cheer me,
He can see me ! he can hear me !
Then the mists of earth would screen us ;
Then the darkness stepped between us.
Still your dear soul I could see,
Suffering yet its way to me.
Pain at last has cut the tether ;
Death will let us live together.
Darling throw your arms around me !
You have found me—you have found me.

Naught on earth had power—had art—
Long to hold us two apart.
None but God were equal to it,
And I knew He would not do it.
Listen ! Hear the echoes swell !
'T is our merry wedding bell.''

LOVE.

LOVE, dear friend, is a sacred thing,
  Love is not tinsel, silver, or gold :
It is a fragment of Heaven's own gate,
  Broken in halves by God's hand, Fate,
And given two kindred spirits bold
  Who would colonize in our Earth unknown :
  'T is whispered them : You may be thrown
Far apart ; be passion-whirled
To different sides of that dizzy world ;
But search for each other, far and near,
With a painful hope, and a joyful fear.
Search through fair or stormy weather,
  Until the halves of this broken gem
Cling and clasp and weld together
  With the power that attracted them.

EDGAR FAWCETT.

I SHALL prize my past, though its light will
    seem
As the flash of a bird's wing seen afar,
For old love remembers young love's dream
As twilight remembers the morning star!

The House on the Hill.

D'OUTRE MORT.

AND so 't is over at last.
        The passion and pain are past;
Death has him and holds him fast!

And now in the chamber dumb
Of his death-sleep, white and numb,
Who of all earth should come

To look on him where he lies,
With her two cold stars of eyes,
And sigh the commonplace sighs,—

Who should stand by his bed,
In her sadness so well-bred,
With just the right poise of head,

But she, this woman he bore,
Through life till life was o'er,
Such infinite longing for?

And now she stands by his bed,
Forgetting to try to shed
One tear, as she sees the dead.

And when those about her fare
From the room, with solemn air
She follows, leaving him there.

But just as she nears the door
There drops on the shadowed floor
A sweet rich rose that she wore.

It drops, and she does not know,
And so lets it lie, and so
Goes out as the others go.

*   *   *   *   *   *

Now they that next draw near
This man, in his sleep austere,
Find, shrinking away with fear,

That a rose, once bright and bland,
Is crushed in his frigid hand. . . .
And they cannot understand!

DECEIVED.

OFTEN I marvel : has she learned at last
　　The secret of my memories? Does she miss
No sweetness of love's fervor in my kiss ?
Find in my gaze no shadow of the past?

Glooming her tranquil joy, has there not crept
　　A dim, half-shapen dread lest I withhold
　　Full fealty, and give not gold for gold,
One spirit lavishing what **one** has kept?

Shall her pure thought serve steadfast, while it
　　　lives,
　　That faultless faith which questions not my
　　　own,
　　Nor ever dream that I have merely shown
Love's meagre semblance for the love she gives?

Shall not unpitying truth, **in future** years,
　　Lay bare the mercy of my falsehood?—Peace,
　　Too timid heart ; a truth like hers shall cease
With life alone ! Assuage thy foolish fears.

Doubt's cruel whisper shall not break the spell,
　　O thou, whom to deceive is to befriend ;
　　All shall be well with thee until the end,
Until the end believing all is well ! !

JAMES JEFFREY ROCHE.

DON'T

YOUR eyes were made for laughter,
    Sorrow befits them not;
Would you be blithe hereafter,
    Avoid the lover's lot.

The rose and lily blended
    Possess your cheeks so fair;
Care never was intended
    To leave his furrows there.

Your heart was not created
    To fret itself away,
Being unduly mated
    To common human clay.

But hearts were made for loving—
    Confound philosophy!
Forget what I 've been proving,
    Sweet Phyllis, and love me.

12

IF.

OH, if the world were mine, Love,
    I 'd give the world for thee !
Alas ! there is no sign, Love,
    Of that contingency.

Were I a king—which is n't
    To be considered now—
A diadem had glistened
    Upon thy lovely brow.

Had Fame with laurels crowned me,—
    She has n't up to date,—
Nor time nor change had found me
    To love and thee ingrate.

If Death threw down his gage, Love,
    Though life is dear to me,
I 'd die, e'en of old age, Love,
    To win a smile from thee.

But being poor we part, Dear,
    And love, sweet love, must die—
Thou wilt not break thy heart, Dear,
    No more, I think, shall I.

FRANCES HODGSON BURNETT.

A WOMAN'S REASON.

I HAVE a reason now for all I do,
A reason that 's so sweet, so old, so new,—
Well, if you were not quite so near to-day,
Or if you 'd turn your eyes another way—
And while I let my hand a moment rest
With clinging touch yet light upon your breast
I might pretend that it was half a jest,
I think perhaps—I 'd tell you.

'T is this,—No, turn your eyes another way,
'T is easier so when what one has to say
Is half pretence—yet somehow makes one's
heart
Stir in one's side, with such a soft, quick start.
'T is this—the old World has been born again,
Born with a strange, sweet, bitter throe of pain,
The sad old World I treated with disdain
Is new because—I love you.

In time gone by did seasons come and go?
And was there summer rain and winter snow?
Perhaps! What matter? Now the violet 's blue,
The rose blooms red—and friends are tried and
true,

The blossoms on the boughs are white in spring,
The wind is soft, **the** birds spread joyous wing,
And soar and wheel in the blue sky—and sing,
    Because—because—I love you.

I scarcely know my own face in the glass,
It almost seems to mock me as I pass,
Once of its few poor beauties **I** was vain,
Now they can only rouse me to disdain,
I should be twenty thousand times as fair,
The stars and sun should light my eyes and
    hair—
And yet—sometimes I think I only care,
    Because—because—I love **you.**

I am so changeful and so full of mood,
Sometimes I would not—and sometimes—I
    would,
I 'm proud and humble, scornful, thoughtful,
    light,
A hundred times between the morn and night,
I cast you off—I try to draw you near,
I hold you lightly—and I hold you dear,
And **all the** time I know with **joy, with** fear,
    It is—because—I love you !

Will you remember this when I seem cold?
When what I yearn to tell is all untold—
When I am wayward, wilful, silent, **proud,**

When if I dared to think my thoughts aloud
They would repeat my jesting—of to-day,
"**A** woman's reason—and a woman's way,
    It is—because—I love you !"

There is a reason now for life and death,
A reason **why** one's heart beats and one's breath
Comes quicker at the light touch of a hand,
My reason makes it summer in the land,
Once from **all pain** I longed all earth to free,
But now there **is a** reason Pain should be,
Since some day **I** might bear it patiently
    Because—because—I **love you.**

And now—my hand clings **closer to your breast,**
Bend your head lower while I say the rest,
The greatest change of all is this—that I,
Who used to be so cold, **so** fierce, so shy,
In the sweet moment **that** I feel you near,
Forget **to be** ashamed, and know no fear,
Forget that Life is sad and Death is drear,
    Because—because—I love you !

IF.

IF he had known that when her proud, **fair**
    face
  Turned from him calm and slow,
Beneath its cold indifference **had** place
  A passionate, deep woe.

If **he** had known that when her hand lay still,
　　Pulseless so near his own,
It was because pain's bitter, bitter chill
　　Changed her to very stone.

If he had known that she had borne so much
　　For sake of the sweet past,
That mere despair said : "This cold **look** and
　　　　touch
　　Must be the cruel last."

If he had known her eyes **so** cold and bright,
　　Watching the sunset's red,
Held back within their deeps of purple light
　　A storm **of tears** unshed.

If he had known the keenly barbèd jest,
　　With such hard lightness thrown,
Cut through the hot, proud heart within her
　　　　breast
　　Before **it** pierced his own.

If she **had known that** when her calm glance
　　　　swept
　　Him as she passed him by,
His blood was fire, **his** pulses madly leapt
　　Beneath her **careless eye.**

If she **had known** that when he touched her
　　　　hand.
　　And felt it still and cold,

There closed round his wrung heart the iron
    band
  Of misery untold.

If she had known that when her laughter rang
  In scorn of sweet past days,
His very soul shook with a deadly pang
  Before her light dispraise.

If she had known that every poisoned dart,
  If she had understood
That each sunk to the depths of his man's heart
  And drew the burning blood.

If she had known that when in the wide west
  The sun sank gold and red,
He whispered bitterly : "'T is like the rest,
  The warmth and light have fled."

If she had known the longing and the pain,
  If she had only guessed,—
One look—one word—and she perhaps had lain
  Silent upon his breast.

If she had known how oft when their eyes met,
  And his so fiercely shone,
But for man's shame and pride they had been
    wet,—
  Ah ! if she had but known !

If they had known the wastes lost love must
    cross,—
  The wastes of unlit lands,—
If they had known what seas of salt tears toss
  Between the barren strands,

If they had known **how** lost **love** prays **for**
    death
  And makes low, ceaseless moan,
Yet never fails his sad, sweet, wearying breath—
  Ah ! if they had but known.

YESTERDAY AND TO-DAY.

YESTERDAY.

IT is so wide, this great world vaulted o'er
  By the blue sky clasping white shore to
    shore.
And yet it is not wide enough for me !
I love you so—it cannot hold my love.
There is not space in earth or heaven above.
There is not room for my great love and me.

TO-DAY.

It is **so** wide, this great world vaulted o'er
By the sad sky clasping dark shore to shore,
It is too wide—it **is** too wide for me !
Would God that **it** were narrowed to a grave,
And I slept quiet, naught hid with me save
The love that was too great—too great for me.

ROBERT BURNS WILSON.

EXTRACT FROM "CONSTANCE."

DO I remember?   Ask me not again :
    My heart hath but one passion—to forget.
Oh, is there nothing in the world, then,
    To take away but once the soul's regret !
Alas ! for love is ever more divine ;
    Immortal is the sorrow love must bring ;
The golden cup aches for withholden wine ;
    Of sun-kissed flight still dreams the broken
        wing ;
The buried jewel seeketh yet to shine,
    And music's spirit haunts the idle string :
So doth the heart in sadness ever twine
    Some fading wreath that keeps hope lingering.
Remember not, my soul, remember not !
    There is a madness lurks in memory.
She hath her music, and the strain once caught
    Forever must the silent wings of thought
Bear to thine ears the mournful threnody.

Bright! is the sky to-day and fair above me :
Hearest thou me, oh ! hearest thou me ?
*Light is my heart to-day, for I **do** love thee ;*
Hearest thou me, my lover ?

White is the bloom of the apple fair,
Sweet is the smell of the clover,
Soft is the kiss of the wanton air;
But love is best,
True love is best:
Ah! hearest thou that, my lover?

Thus ran the song, and she who sang that day,
    No other seemed but God's own masterpiece.

    *   *   *   *   *   *

Fair were the fields to-day and thou hadst
    found me:
Hearest thou me, oh! hearest thou me?
Sweet were the bonds of love and thou hadst
    bound me:
Hearest thou me, my lover?
Sweet is the sound of the red-breast's song
When the owl flies out from cover,
Sweetest is, sleep if the day be long,
But love is best—
Get thee to my breast:
Ah! hearest thou that, my lover?

A SONG.

I DO not ask—dear love—not I,
    A jeweled crown to win,
Nor robe, nor crown—nor do I cry
To those that guard the gates of heaven,
    That they should let me in.

Oh, when they talk of far-off strands,
  I have no heart to pray,
So lonely seem those heavenly lands,
I feel no wish for angel hands
  To wipe my tears away.

I care not for the joyous throng,
  My soul could never share
The endless bliss—the happy song ;
How long the days, O God, how long,
  If I should miss thee there !

Nay, love ; I only could be blest
  Close by thy side to be,
To hold thy hand—to lean at rest,
Forever on thy faithful breast,
  That would be heaven for me.

ARLO BATES.

ONE.

THE world is naught till one is come
  Who is the world ; then beauty wakes,
And voices sing that have been dumb.

The world is naught when one is gone
  Who was the world ; then the heart breaks
That this is lost which once was won.

Dear love, this life, so passion-fraught,
  From you its bliss or sorrow takes ;
With you is all ; without you naught.

A FANTASY.

IF there were a thousand years
    Between my life and me,
And as in an age-dim tome
  I might its story see,—

How mystic and sweet and strange,
    Like some old tale, would be
The anguish that now I know
    In my hopeless love for thee !

A RECOGNITION.

LOVER and mistress, sleeping side by side,
    Death smote at once ; and in the outer air,
Amazedly confronted, each to each,
    Their spirits stood, of all disguises bare.

With sudden loathing stung, one spirit fled,
    Crying, " Love turns to hate if this be thou ! "
" Ah, stay ! " the other wailed, in swift pursuit,
    " Thee I have never truly loved till now ! "

H. C. BUNNER.

CANDOR.

" I KNOW what you are going to say," she
    said,
  And she stood up, looking uncommonly tall ;
  "You are going to speak of the hectic fall,
And say you are sorry the summer 's dead.
  And no other summer was like it, you know,
  And can I imagine what made it so ?
Now, are n't you honestly ?" "Yes," I said.

"I know what you are going to say," she said.
  "You are going to ask if I forget
  That day in June when the woods were wet,
And you carried me "—here she dropped her
        head—
  "Over the creek ; you are going to say
  Do I remember that horrid day,
Now, are n't you honestly ?" "Yes," I said.

"I know what you are going to say," she said.
  "You are going to say that since that time,
  You have rather tended to run to rhyme,

And ”—her clear glance fell and her cheek grew
     red—
  “And have I noticed your tone was queer?—
  Why, everybody has seen it here!—
Now, are n't you honestly?” “Yes,” I said.

“I know what you are going to say,” I said.
  “You are going to say you 've been much
    annoyed,
  And I 'm short of tact—you will say devoid—
And I 'm clumsy and awkward, and call me
    Ted,
  And I bear abuse like a dear old lamb,
  And you 'll have me any way, just as I am,
Now, are n't you honestly?” “Ye-es,” she said.

FROM “THE WAY TO ARCADY.”

WHAT know you not, old man (quoth he)—
  Your hair is white, your face is wise—
That Love must kiss that mortal's eyes
Who hopes to see fair Arcady?
No gold can buy you entrance there,
But beggared Love may go all bare—
No wisdom won with weariness;
But Love goes in with Folly's dress—
No fame that wit could ever win;
But only Love may lead Love in
  To Arcady, to Arcady.

Ah, woe is me! through all my days
  Wisdom and wealth I both have got,
And fame, and name, and great men's praise,
  But Love, ah, Love! I have it not.
There was a time when life was new—
  But far away and half forgot—
I only know her eyes were blue;
  But Love—I fear I knew it not.
We did not wed, for lack of gold,
And she is dead and I am old.
All things have come since then to me,
Save Love, oh, Love! and Arcady.

Ah, then I fear we part (quoth he),
My way 's for Love and Arcady.

But you, you fare alone, like me;
  The gray is likewise in your hair.
  What love have you to lead you there?
To Arcady, to Arcady?

Ah, no, not lonely do I fare;
  My true companion's Memory.
With love he fills the spring-time air;
  With love he clothes the winter tree.
Oh, past this poor horizon's bound,
  My song goes straight to one who stands—
Her face all gladdening at the sound—
  To lead me to the spring-green lands,
  To wander with enlacing hands.

The songs within my heart that stir
Are all of her, are all of her.
My maid is dead long years (quoth he),
She waits for me in Arcady.

HOMER GREENE.

WHAT MY LOVER SAID.

BY the merest chance, in the twilight gloom,
  In the orchard path he met me;
In the tall wet grass, with its faint perfume,
And I tried to pass, but he made no room,
  Oh! I tried, but he would not let me.
So I stood and blushed till the grass grew red,
  With my face bent down above it,
While he took my hand, as he whispering said—
(How the clover lifted each pink, sweet head.
To listen to all that my lover said;
  Oh, the clover in bloom, I love it!)

In the high wet grass went the path to hide,
  And the low wet leaves hung over;
But I could not pass upon either side,
For I found myself, when I vainly tried,
  In the arms of my steadfast lover.
And he held me there and he raised my head,
  While he closed the path before me,

And he looked down into my eyes and said—
(How the leaves bent down from the boughs
        o'erhead
To listen to all that my lover said ;
    Oh ! the leaves hanging lowly o'er me !)

Had he moved aside but a little way
    I could surely then have passed him ;
And he knew I never could wish to stay,
And would not have heard what he had to say,
    Could I only aside have cast him.
It was almost dark, and the moments sped,
    And the searching night-wind found us,
But he drew me nearer and softly said—
(How the pure, sweet wind grew still, instead,
To listen to all that my lover said ;
    Oh ! the whispering wind around us !)

I am sure that he knew when he held me fast,
    That I must be all unwilling ;
For I tried to go, and I would have passed,
As the night was come with its dew at last,
    And the sky with its stars was filling.
But he clasped me close, when I would have
        fled,
    And he made me hear his story,
And his soul came out from his lips and said—
(How the stars crept out when the white moon
        led,

To listen to all that my lover said ;
  Oh, the moon and stars in glory !)

I know that the grass and leaves will not tell,
  And I 'm sure that the wind, precious rover,
Will carry his secret so safely and well
  That no being will ever discover
One word of the many that rapidly fell
  From the soul-speaking lips of my lover ;
  And the moon and the stars that looked over
Shall never reveal what a fairy-like spell
They wove round about us that night in the dell,
  In the path through the dew-laden clover,
Nor echo the whispers that made my heart
    swell,
  As they fell from the lips of my lover.

MIZPAH.

" The Lord watch between me and thee, when we are
absent one from another."— Genesis xxxi, 49.

I KISSED your lips and held your hands,
  And said, " Farewell," and went away,
  Well knowing that another day
Would speed you forth to other lands.
  And down the summer-scented street
  I heard your echoing voice repeat
  The Hebrew motto, quaint and sweet—
    " Mizpah."

A thousand miles between us lay
  When Autumn passed, iu lingering flight,
  And drenched with fragrant dew at night
The woodland fires he lit by day ;
  But, all the golden distance through,
  From you to me and me to you
  Went out the tender prayer and true—
        " Mizpah."

The winter night falls cold and bleak ;
  I sit, in saddened mood, alone,
  And listen to the wind's low moan,
And hide a fear I dare not speak.
  For you are far, so far away,
  And younger lips have turned to clay :
  Dear love ! I tremble while I pray,
        " Mizpah."

But spring shall blossom up the plain,
  And Easter lilies scent the air,
  And song-birds riot everywhere,
And heart and hope grow glad again.
  Yet still my nightly prayer shall be,
  Though swallows build or swallows flee,
  Until my love come back to me,
        " Mizpah."

And when, with flowers of June, you come,
  And face to face again we stand,

And heart to heart and hand to hand,
O love ! within the one dear home,
We shall not need to say again,
In winter's snow or summer's rain,
Till death shall come to part us **twain,**
" Mizpah."

JAMES WHITCOMB RILEY.

WHEN **SHE** COMES HOME.

WHEN she comes home again ! **A thou-**
    sand ways
I fashion to myself, the tenderness
Of my glad welcome : I shall tremble—yes ;
And touch her, as when first in the old days
I touched her girlish hand, nor dared upraise
    Mine eyes, such was my faint heart's sweet
        distress.
    Then silence : And the perfume of her dress :
    The room will sway a little, and a haze
Cloy eyesight—soulsight, even,—for a space :
    And tears—yes ; and the ache here in the
        throat.
    To know that **I** so ill-deserve the place
Her arms make for me ; and the sobbing **note**
    I stay with kisses, ere the tearful face
    Again is hidden in the old embrace.

THE DEAD LOVER.

TIME is so long when a man is dead !
　　Some one sews ; and the room is made
Very clean ; and the light is shed
　　Softly through the window shade.

Yesterday I thought :　" I know
　　Just how the bells will sound, and how
The friends will talk, and the sermon go,
　　And the hearse-horse bow and bow !"

This is to-day ; and I have no thing
　　To think of—nothing whatever to do
But to hear the throb of the pulse of a wing
　　That wants to fly back to you.

MAURICE FRANCIS EGAN.

THE ANXIOUS LOVER.

I SAW a damsel in a sombre room,
　　Laid low in beds of purple violet,
And　pale,　sweet roses,　that perfumed　the
　　gloom ;
And then I thought : This is a gray sunset

Of days of loving life.   Shall he who stands
  Beside her bier, in sorrow for his love,
Be first in Heaven to clasp her gentle hands,
  To bow with her before the Lord **above?**

If love can die, let my heart be as cold
  As Galatea's was before the words
Of the warm sculptor drew it from the **mold**
  And made her hear the sound **of singing**
    birds.
Love's sunshine **and** love's shadows are they
    all
  Like April sun **and** shadow on the earth?
If love can die at sight of funeral-pall,
  Would I had strangled it in its sad birth.

I know that the sweet Spring will surely go,
  And leave no trace, except a blossom dry ;
I know that life will pass as passes snow
  When March winds blow and river-floods **are**
    high ;
I know that all the maples on the hill,
  That fire the air with flame, to ashes burn ;
I know that all the singing birds that fill
  The air with song to silent dust will turn.

Oh ! love, my love, can **it**, then, ever be
  That thou or I may gaze upon love's death ?

That thou shalt some day, sad and silently,
  Look on me dumb and cold and without
      breath?
Or, shall I see thee lying white and wan,
  Like yonder damsel in the flower-bed,
And only say: "My lady sweet has gone;
  She 's lost to me; she 's dead; *what meaneth
      dead?* "

If love can die, then I will no more look
  Into thy eyes, and see thy pure thoughts
      there,
Nor will I read in any poet's book
  Of all the things that poets make so fair.
If love can die, the poet's art is vain,
  And thy blue eyes might well be blossoms
      blue,
And thy soft tears be only senseless rain,
  Since love can die, like flowers and soulless
      dew.

I care not for thy smile, if love can die.
  If I must leave thee, let me leave thee now.
Shall I not know thee, if in Heaven high
  I enter and before the Holy bow?
Shalt thou not know me when before the throne
  Thou, white-robed one, shalt enter into light?
I cannot think the Lord of Love has sown
  His precious seed to make but one day bright.

Would I were dead, if death is then the end
  Of all the loving that makes life so fair.
If love can die, I pray the sun may send
  An arrow through my head, that death may
    tear
Away my soul, and make me soon forget
  The fair, false hope of an eternal dawn,
Which yet may die like purple violet
  Strewn on the robe of that sweet damsel wan.

Ah ! love, my love, when I look in thy eyes,
  And hear thy voice, like softened village-bells,
Coming to one who long has sent up sighs
  From foreign lands to be where his love
    dwells,
My heart lifts up itself in ecstasy.
  " Life were not life if our strong love could die.
The earth may crumble, but our love and **we**
  Shall live forever.   This is true ! " I cry.

LIKE A LILAC.

LIKE a lilac in the spring
    Is my love, my lady-love ;
Purple-white, the lilacs fling
    Scented blossoms from above :
So my love, my lady-love,
    Throws soft glances on my heart ;
Ah, my dainty lady-love,
    Every glance is Cupid's dart.

Like a pansy in the spring
  Is my love, my lady-love ;
For her velvet eyes oft bring
  Golden fancies from above :
Ah, my heart is pansy-bound
  By those eyes so tender-true ;
Balmy heart's-ease have I found,
  Dainty lady-love in you.

Like the changeful month of spring
  Is my love, my lady-love ;
Sunshine comes and glad birds sing,
  Then a rain-cloud floats above :
So your moods change with the wind,
  April-tempered lady-love ;
All the sweeter, to my mind.
  You 're a riddle, lady-love.

— —

G. HERBERT SASS.

"BARTON GREY."

—

JOAN MELLISH.

WHERE art thou now, Joan Mellish ?
  Spring with its smiles slips past ;
The great red rose in the convent close

Crimsons and glows at last ;
And with the time of roses
  Old hopes new life assume :
Where art thou, then, Joan Mellish ?
  Shall naught thine eyes relume ?

Thy step was free and stately
  As the step of the mountain fawn ;
Thy cheek's faint flush like the rosy blush
  In the first sweet hush of dawn ;
And oh, thy heart, Joan Mellish,
  Was just the truest heart
That ever the dear God sent below
  To bear an earthly part.

I seek for thee, Joan Mellish,
  At morn, at noon, at eve ;
I turn and turn, and pant and burn,
  I strive and yearn and grieve ;
But not for sigh or whisper,
  For passionate sob or cry,
Dost thou come back, my love, my life !
  And still the years go by.

Thou wilt not come, Joan Mellish,
  Thy feet the earth-dust holds ;
Where strangers pass the long grave-grass
  Thy couch, alas, **enfolds.**
And I, thine earthly lover,—

Ah me, how far am I
From that dark home of thine below,
  From thy bright home on high !

But as the twilight deepens,
  Where'er my footsteps stray,
I seek thee still by vale and hill,
  By lake and rill and bay :
But still the earth is empty,
  And still my heart is sore,
Because thy face, Joan Mellish,
  Shines on me nevermore.

Ah me, the bitter parting
  Of love that is not hope !
Farewell for aye, dear heart !   Astray
  In doubt's dark way I grope ;
My eyes are dim with seeking
  The face they cannot see.
Farewell, farewell, Joan Mellish,
  A long farewell to thee !

A SUMMER CLOUD.

A VEIL of mist is drawn across the billow
  Out yonder where the night and day have
    met
And the sea bird on his restless, foamy pillow
  Broods silent where the summer sun has set ;

In their leafy home in yonder oak the swallows
  Are resting **from** the chatter of the day,
And the broken star-beams glimmer **in the**
    hollows
  Of the scarcely heaving waters of the bay.

The outer stillness steals in through the casement
  And falls as with a spell upon our lips,
And the sadness of a sudden deep abasement
  Comes o'er me like a shadow of eclipse.
And I look upon you sitting silent by me,
  As one by one the stars grow bright above,
And wonder what great trial waits to try me
  And fit me for the treasure of your love.

I have loved you, O my darling ! with **a** passion
  Too absolute to dread its own unworth ;
I have lavished all my life in reckless fashion,
  Nor counted what the moments should **bring**
    forth.
And now at last, when all the doubt is over,
  And that dear heart has nestled in my own,
Do you wonder that I pause—your human
    lover ?
  Do you marvel that so **grave my eyes have**
    grown ?

Ah ! well, I will not teach you all the reason,
  Nor whisper the sad secret of thy pain.
What heart that ever loved but had its season

Of passionate, impulsive self-disdain ?
I only see your dear eyes shining on me,
  I only feel the trouble pass and cease,
And bow beneath the gentle grace that won me,
  And clasp again my talisman of peace.

And verily, my darling, as you sit there
  So unconscious, with your cheek upon your
      hand,
While the deepening shadows round you glide
      and flit there,
  I think that now at last I understand
All the power and the blessing and the glory
  That lifts the faithful spirit far above
The troubles of life's sad and stormy story,
  The magic of the mighty name of Love.

On the blue bay's placid bosom over yonder
  The harbor lights gleam dimly far and near ;
Back and forth and up and down the slow waves
      wander,
  And the surf-beat echoes faintly in my ear ;
And through the darkness, timidly and slowly,
  Your little hand steals softly into mine ;
And lo ! on yonder cloud-bank couching lowly,
  Love sets his star before us for a sign.

DEFEAT.

HE took her hand and looked at her,
  No sound did that deep stillness stir ;

Even the weary wandering rain
Had ceased to beat upon the pane ;
Only about the wistful mouth
A sigh, more faint than the faint South,
Hovered a moment's space, and then
Died into nothingness again.

The words he spoke were brief and slow :—
What could he say she did not know !
What pulse **of** that impetuous soul
But owned **her** calm, serene **control?**
No need for **him to** test her heart
With cunning fence of verbal art ;
Only **to ask and** wait her will,
And, winning—losing—love her still.

Perhaps she wavered ; ay, perhaps
The shadow **of** the cloud that wraps
The future from our questioning gaze
Let **in some** glimpse of after days :—
Some hint of all she might possess
In that true spirit's tenderness,
If but her weaker life might move
Unto the music of his love.

Perhaps ! Who knows ? **He only knew**
The great grey eyes were **dim** with dew ;
Saw only on the mouth's sweet bloom
The shadow of reluctant doom ;

Felt only one sad, gentle word——
And then, through that deep stillness heard
Once more the weary, wandering rain
Beat dull against the window pane.

SUSAN MARR SPAULDING.

DEATH'S FIRST LESSON.

THREE sad, strange things already death hath
    shown
To me who lived but yesterday.   My love
Who loved to kiss my hands and lips above
All other joys,—whose heart upon my own
So oft has throbbed,—fears me, now life has
    flown,
And shuddering turns away.   The friend who
    strove
My trust to win, and all my faith did prove,
Sees, in my pale, still form, a bar o'erthrown
To some most dear desire.   While one who
    spake
No fond and flattering word of love or praise,
Who only cold and stern reproof would give
To all my foolish, unconsidered ways—
This one would glad have died that I might
    live,
This heart alone lies broken for my sake.

FATE.

TWO shall be born the **whole wide world**
    apart,
And speak in different tongues, and have no
    thought
Each of the other's being, and no heed;
And these, o'er unknown seas to unknown
    lands
Shall cross, escaping wreck, defying death;
And all unconsciously shape every act
And bend each wandering **step to** this one
    end—
That, one day, out of darkness they shall meet,
And read life's meaning in each other's eyes.

And two shall walk some narrow way of life,
So nearly side by side, that should one turn
Ever so little to the left or right,
They needs must stand acknowledged face to
    face,
And yet with wistful eyes that never meet,
With groping hands that never clasp, and lips
Calling in vain to ears that never hear,
They seek each other all their weary days,
And die unsatisfied—and this is Fate.

JOSEPHINE POLLARD.

OPPOSITES.

FIRE.

THE heat of a thousand summers
　　With passion inflames my blood,
And the spirit of countless demons
　　Pours through my veins like a flood;
Oh, never were kisses hotter
　　Than those on her lips I press,
And vainly would Love dissemble
　　The fervor of my caress.
Swiftly I work my will,
　　And none can deny my power;
Love has its lessons from me,
　　And where I love I devour!

FROST.

As cold as sierra's crest
　　Are the seas in **my** breast congealed:
By me the passions of life
　　Are cooled, and its wounds concealed.
From the grasp of a lurid foe
　　My touch is a swift release,
And over the banners of war
　　I broider the lilies of peace.

14

Yet never with more intense
An ardor the lover yearns
Than **I** when the flame within
To a passionate white-heat burns.
E'en as a thief in the night
I steal in the presence of joy ;
Love turneth chill at my breath,
For where I love I destroy !

LOVE'S POWER.

IF I were blind, and thou shouldst enter
E'er so softly in the room,
I should know it,
I should feel it,
Something subtle would reveal it,
And a glory round thee centre
That would lighten up the gloom.
And my heart would surely guide me,
With Love's second-sight provide me,
One amid the crowd to find,
If I were blind !

If I were deaf, and thou hadst spoken
Ere thy presence I had known,
I should know it,
I should feel it,
Something subtle would reveal it,

And the seal at once be broken
By Love's liquid undertone.
Deaf to other, stranger voices,
And the world's discordant noises,—
Whisper, wheresoe'er thou art,
    'T will reach my heart !

If I were dead, and thou shouldst venture
  Near the coffin where I lay,
    I should know it,
    I should feel it,
  Something subtle would reveal it,
  And no look of mildest censure
  Rest upon that face of clay.
  Shouldst thou kiss me, conscious flashes
  Of Love's fire through Death's cold ashes
  Would give back the cheek its red,
    If I were dead !

ELLA WHEELER WILCOX.

WHAT LOVE IS.

LOVE is the centre and circumference ;
  The cause and aim of all things—'t is the
    key
To joy and sorrow, and the recompense
  For all the ills that have been, or may be.

Love is as bitter as the dregs of sin,
  As sweet as clover-honey in its cell;
Love is the password whereby souls get in
  To Heaven—the gate that leads, sometimes,
    to Hell.

Love is the crown that glorifies; the curse
  That brands and burdens; it is life and death.
It is the great law of the universe;
  And nothing can exist without its breath.

Love is the impulse which directs the world,
  And all things know it and obey its power.
Man, in the maelstrom of his passions whirled;
  The bee that takes the pollen to the flower;

The earth, uplifting her bare, pulsing breast
  To fervent kisses of the amorous sun;—
Each but obeys creative Love's behest,
  Which everywhere instinctively is done.

Love is the only thing that pays for birth,
  Or makes death welcome. Oh, dear God
    above
This beautiful but sad, perplexing earth,
  Pity the hearts that know—or know not—
    Love!

FROM "COULEUR DE ROSE."

OH, rapture—promise of the May,
  Oh, June, fulfilling after !
If Autumn sighs when Summer dies,
  'T is drowned in Winter's laughter.
Oh, maiden dawns—oh, wifely noons,
  Oh, siren sweet, sweet nights !
I 'd want no Heaven could earth be given
  Again with its delights,
      (If love stayed near).

IMPATIENCE.

HOW can I wait until you come to me ?
    The once fleet mornings linger by the
  way ;
Their sunny smiles touched with malicious glee
  At my unrest, they seem to pause and play
  Like truant children, while I sigh and say,
      How can I wait ?

How can I wait? Of old, the rapid hours
  Refused to pause or loiter with me long ;
But now they idly fill my hands with flowers,
  And make no haste, but slowly stroll among
  The summer blooms, not heeding my one
    song,
      How can I wait ?

How can I wait? The nights alone are kind ;
They reach forth to a future day, and bring
Sweet dreams of you to people all my mind,
  And time speeds by on light and airy wing.
  I feast upon your face, I no more sing,
          How can **I** wait?

How can I wait? The morning breaks the spell
  A pitying night has flung upon my soul.
You are not near me, and I know full well
  My heart has need of patience and control ;
  Before we meet, hours, days, and weeks must
    roll,
        How can **I wait?**

How can I wait? Oh, love, how can I wait
  Until the sunlight of your eyes shall shine
Upon my world that seems so desolate?
  Until your hand-clasp warms my blood like
    wine ;
Until you come again, O love of mine,
        How can I wait?

AD FINEM.

ON the white throat of the useless passion
    That scorched my soul with its burning
    breath,
I clutched my fingers in murderous fashion
    And gathered them close in a grip of death ;

For why should I fan, or feed with fuel,
  A love that showed me but blank despair?
So my hold was firm, and my grasp was cruel—
  I meant to strangle it then and there!

I thought it was dead.   But with no warning
  It rose from its grave last night, and came
And stood by my bed till the early morning,
  And over and over it spoke your name.
Its throat was red where my hands had held it,
  It burned my brow with its scorching breath;
And I said, the moment my eyes beheld it,
  "A love like this can know no death."

For just one kiss that your lips have given
  In the lost and beautiful past to me,
I would gladly barter my hopes of Heaven
  And all the bliss of Eternity.
For never a joy are the angels keeping
  To lay at my feet in Paradise,
Like that of into your strong arms creeping
  And looking into your love-lit eyes.

I know in the way that sins are reckoned,
  This thought is a sin of the deepest dye;
But I know, too, if an angel beckoned,
  Standing close by the Throne on High,
And you adown by the gates infernal,
  Should open your loving arms and smile,

I would turn my back on things supernal,
  To lie on your breast a little while.

To know for an hour you were mine completely—
  Mine in body and soul, my own—
I would bear unending tortures sweetly,
  With not a murmur and not a moan.
A lighter sin or a lesser error
  Might change through hope or fear divine ;
But there is no fear, and hell has no terror
  To change or alter a love like mine.

THE WAY OF IT.

THIS is the way of it, wide world over,
  One is beloved and one is the lover,
One gives and the other receives.
One lavishes all in a wild emotion,
One offers a smile for a life's devotion,
  One hopes and the other believes.
One lies awake in the night to weep,
And the other drifts off in a sweet sound sleep.

One soul is aflame with a Godlike passion,
One plays with love in an idler's fashion,
  One speaks and the other hears.
One sobs " I love you," and wet eyes show it,
And one laughs lightly, and says, " I know it,"
  With smiles for the other's tears.

One lives for the other and nothing beside,
And the other remembers the world is wide.

This is the way of it, sad earth over,
The heart that breaks is the heart of the lover,
  And the other learns to forget.
"For what is the use of endless sorrow,
Though the sun goes down, it will rise to-mor-
    row ;
  And life is not over yet?"
Oh ! I know this truth, if I know no other,
That passionate Love is Pain's own mother.

ANNA C. PALMER.

(MRS. GEORGE ARCHIBALD.)

QUIT YOUR FOOLIN'.

Girls is queer ! I use' to think
  Emmy did n't care for me,
For whenever I would try
  Any lovin' arts, to see
How she 'd take 'em—sweet or sour,—
  Always, saucy-like, says she :
        "Quit your foolin' !"

Once, agoin' home from church,
  Just to find if it would work,
Round her waist I slipped my arm,—
  My! You 'd ought 'o seen her jerk,
Spunky? Well, she acted so—
And she snapped me up as perk—
          "Quit your foolin'!"

Ev'ry time 't wuz jest the same,
  Till one night I says, says I,
Chokin' some I must admit,
  Tremblin' some I don't deny,—
"Emmy, seein' 's I don't suit,
  Guess I better say 'good-bye,'
          An' quit foolin'.' "

Girls is queer! **She only** laughed,—
  Cheeks all dimplin'; "John," says she,
" Foolin' men that never gits
  Real in earnest, ain't for me."
Wa' n't that cute? I took the hint,
  An' a chair, and staid, an' we
          Quit our foolin'!

HER COMPANY.

WHEN ma **died I** wuz only jest
  Fourteen, but older than the rest.
'T wuz New-Year day she went away
An' left an achin' in my breast.

It seemed so cheerless like to me
Without my mother's company.

Says pa : " They 's no one I kin get
Kin do as well as **you**, Janet."
So school an' fun fer me wuz done,
An' still I managed not to fret.
The young ones thrived, an' as fer me,
I 'd Jim an' work **fer** company.

Poor Jim wuz lame, an' that wuz why
I always had him settin' by.
His lovin' ways made glad the days,
Till all at once he had to die.
The neighbors they wuz glad fer **me**—
But how I missed his company !

I worked along ; **the** children dear,
They married off from **year to** year.
"**An'** one cold night **at** candle-light,
Says pa : " It 's purty lonesome here,
An' New-Year you shall have," says he,
" A nice, new ma, fer company ! "

He laughed an' set an' talked awhile,
But, as fer me, I could n't smile.
An' all night long my tears run down,
As I lay rasslin' with my trial.
I wisht that I, like Jim, could be
In my dead mother's company.

It 's odd how things turns out ; next day
In walked our neighbor, Zenas Gray.
My eyes wuz red, an' Zenas said :
"Janet been cryin'? What 's to pay ? "
"Oh, nothin' much," says I. Says he :
" I reckon you need company."

An' after that he ust to come,
An' cheer me up if I wuz glum.
An' when he went I 'd feel content,
An' work an' sing or set an' hum.
The empty house, it seemed to me,
Wuz full of his good company.

An' every thought of ma an' Jim,
Would somehow make me think of him.
It brought relief to bygone grief,
An' filled my heart up to the brim,
Especial, when he offered me
Himself for stiddy **company.**

An' now, with hope in by **an'** by,
As New-Year time is drawin' nigh,
The tears I shed **fer them** that 's dead
Ain't sech as when **I ust** to cry.
I only trust that **they kin see**
How I enjoy my company.

WASTE.

I.

TO one he sent his strong man's heart laid
    bare,
Quivering with hope and fear. A cruel hand
Seemed pressing hard upon a torn, hot nerve,
Nothing he kept, not even his fierce pride.
Unfaithful to another—to her true,
Complete surrender of his heart and life.

II.

The second letter was indifferent,
Save for an old-time name he knew she **loved :**
He snatched a fading flower from his coat,
And crushed its purple blood against the words
That she might know, for all his city life,
He still recalled her love for violets !

III.

The one to whom he wrote with lashes wet
(His pleading was so strong and passionate)
Read with fierce scorn his letter—flung it **by—**
And, later, answered in a mocking tone . . .

The other died.   Upon her broken heart
Was found a locket with his face inside—
A tender word cut from his letter—and—a violet.

ESTRANGED.

DO you think, dear Love, if we had **known**
   That, ere another year had flown,
We should have drifted far apart,
We who for years claspt heart to heart,
Do you think we had been more tender?

Ah ! to think this is your natal day,
And I so near, yet miles away?
Why, I could reach you in one short hour,
Yet dare not send you even a flower,
Not even forget-me-nots !

And I used to know your heart so well
That I could look in your eyes and tell
All that was there ; but now, to-day,
If we should meet, you would turn away,
Not letting me see your eyes.

Oh ! If you 'd look just once again.
What should I find there, hate or pain,
Love or longing, or coldness, dear,
Or—how my heart leaps to dream it—a tear
Calling me back again?

DANSKE DANDRIDGE.

PARTED.

OH that I stood in the presence of God !
   In the visible presence of God,
  And had voice for one cry !
That my body were dead and my **soul were**
    alive
  In the light of that palpable eye.

" God, give me one boon for my life
  That was painful and long ;
    For the waiting ; the years—oh, the years !
    For the yearnings and tears ;
  For the hurt and the wrong :—
God grant me one boon **for my** life.

" Somewhere—oh, Thou knowest the where—
  In Thy worlds with their heavens and hells,
In the limitless spaces of **air,**
He *is*, and Thou knowest the where !
A boon, oh, a boon ! Send **me there !**

" For I bore it, the worst that was sent ;
  The pitiless ache of the tears ;

The loss and the fierce discontent,
  And **the** horror and fears
    Of that silence more hard than a **wall** ;
      And the fancies, so maddeningly sweet,
    More cruel than all :—
    By the love that is deathless, **I call,**
      As I fall at thy feet."

Would I cry ?   Would the floods be unsealed
  In that Presence, in sight of the Thrones?
Would I jar the loud joy of the blest
  With my strenuous tones?
Or stand with my hand on my mouth,
  Unable to praise or to pray :
Just *feeling,* " Thou knowest it all,
    What *is* there to say?"

THREE DAYS.

I T was a wild and lonely hill,
    And in the long grass at my **feet**
You lay ; **the** breeze was almost still,
    Poising on airy wings, **and sweet**
With clover-breath **of** resting cows ;
The light fell softly through the boughs ;
That light was **dear for dear** Love's sake :
'T was there our hearts began to wake.

We watched the summer sun arise,
  Standing together on the lawn :
Then turned, and in each other's eyes
  We gazed to watch another dawn.
We felt the radiance of the sun ;
Our day of love was just begun ;
That day was sweet for sweet Pain's sake :
'T was there our hearts began to ache.

They call the old wood Fairyland ;
  I know we lovers loitered there.
'T was nightfall, we were hand in hand,
  The distant thunder stirred the air ;
Your trembling tones were low and deep ;
We smiled, we laughed—lest we should weep ;
Then parted, for dear Honor's sake :
For Honor's sake—for Honor's sake,
That spot is dear for Honor's sake :
'T was there our hearts began to break.

———

CARLOTTA PERRY.

THROUGH TIME AND ETERNITY

I HAVE done at last with the bitter lie,—
  The lie I have lived so many years.
I 've hated myself that I could not die,
  Body as well as soul.   What ! tears?
15

Tears and kisses on lip and brow :—
What use are tears and kisses now ?

'T was not so hard.　Just a kerchief wet
　In the deadly blessing that quiets pain,
And backward the tide of suffering set,
　Peace swept over the blood and brain,—
Utter peace, to the finger-tips ;
And now these kisses on lids and lips.

Sweet caresses for lips all cold,
　And loud laments for perished breath,
For the faded cheek and the hair's wan gold,
　But not a tear for the sadder death
I died that day.　How strange the fate
That brings your sorrow all too late !

All these years, with my dead, dead heart
　I 've met the world with smiling eyes :
I feigned sweet life with perfect art.
　And the world has respect for well-told lies ;
And I fooled the world,—for no one said,
" Behold this woman : she is dead."

And no one said, as you passed along,
　" Behold a murderer."　No one knew :
You carefully covered the cruel wrong :
　That the world saw not, was enough for you,
You had wisdom and worldly pride,
And I had silence,—for I had died.

The world says now I am dead ; but, oh,
  Lean down and listen.   'T is all in vain :
Again in my heart bleeds the cruel blow,
  Again I am mad with the old-time pain,
Again the waves of anguish roll,—
For I have met with my murdered soul.

Oh, never to find the peace I crave,
  'T were better to be as I have been.
In the place of the fleeting years I have
  Eternity now to love you in,
Eternity now to feel the blow
Your dear hands gave in the long ago.

THE BOND OF PAIN.

WHEN the music your soul is filled with
    Flowed out to the world glad and strong,
The heart of the great world was thrilled with
  The delight of your song.
But long ere the world paused to hear it,
  And yet while the dear lips were dumb,
I heard (for my soul was so near it),
The music that burdened your spirit,
  And the songs that should come.

When your ships have come home heavy laden
  With treasures repaying your pains,

The world, from the sage to the maiden,
  Has rejoiced in your gains.
But when, by the storms overtaken,
  Your ships, with their treasures, went down ;
'T was then, by the fair winds forsaken,
At your side, with courage unshaken,
  I faced the world's frown.

Now far in Fame's uttermost regions,
  You stand in the light of the sun ;
And hear the proud voices of legions
  Hail the heights you have won :
But when, by your cares overweighted,
  You wept in the valley alone,
Or groped on the hillside, belated,
My heart with a faith unabated,
  Clasped hands with your own.

You stand in the sunlighted distance
  And I in the Valley of Tears ;
Between us, with weary insistance,
  Lie the merciless years.
But I know, should the tempest surround you,
  For the sound of my voice you would hark ;
Disdaining the hands that would wound you,
You would reach through the dangers around
    you
  For my hand in the dark.

And so, though the great world may claim you,
  And hail you with pleasure and pride,
And so, though I never may name you,
  Who should stand at your side.
Yet O ! my beloved, forever,
  The bond 'twixt us two will remain ;
All time with its utmost endeavor,
  Is powerless to break it in twain ;
Nor yet can eternity sever
  This bond of our Sorrow and Pain.

CHARLES G. BLANDEN.

IN DREAMS AT NIGHT.

IN dreams at night, I often see
  Great proofs of immortality ;—
  The way I tread is grander far
  Than any waking journeys are
To wealth, to fame, or learning's tree.

My soul leaps up, as blissful, free,
  As ever I could wish to be,
    And wings its flight from star to star,
      In dreams at night.

Oh, long and far, I, happy, flee,
Yet still my thoughts turn not from thee;
Thy love—the proof I do unbar,
Thine eyes—the stars, dark Corivar,
That gleam and glow to beacon me
In dreams at night.

THE RACE.

"WE 'll run a race," quoth Thought to
Heart,
"To find a just decree,
If 't is with you Love makes his home,
Or, Kardia dear, with me.

"The goal, my sweet, shall be the mouth,
The eyes the signal give;
Sir Tongue shall then proclaim the seat
Where Love does really live."

That moment passed Diana fair;
Thought leapt the journey o'er,
Too late, too late! the throbbing heart
Was at the goal before.

VALENTINE.

I WOULD I were the little flower
That springeth in thy path;
Its life is one of happiness,
A happy death it hath.

You love it, pluck it, to your lips
 You press the modest eyes,
It closes them and falls asleep :
 That kiss is paradise.

O make me, Sweet, thy valentine,
 Or I that flower shall prove
Which rude winds shatter, pitiless,
 And no lips love.

WILLIAM S. LORD.

IN SIGHT.

LONG years, belovèd, held us far apart ;
 A waste of days, the goal beyond her
  sight,
We only knew by our firm faith in right,
That somehow, some day, bringing heart to
  heart,
Our ways would meet and never more would
  part,
 And we would both be happy, bearing light
 To make life's journey for each other bright,
And knowing balm to heal each burning smart.
But now, oh, joy ! belovèd, see the goal ;

Behold the glory of that mountain peak !
Ah, sweet, your eyes are lit with happy tears,
A light is in them laying bare your soul.
A little while, dear love, and all we seek
Will then be ours, to crown the coming years.

LOVE IS DEAD.

MOAN, ye winds, moan, oh moan,
　(Fog o' th' fen and salt o' th' sea)
Toss ye the trees till they groan,
　(Fog o' th' fen and salt o' th' sea)
　　Love is dead,
　　Tears are shed,
　　Hope has fled ;
Dole ye a dirge with me.

Where have they buried him, wind ;
　(Fog o' th' fen and salt o' th' sea)
Search through the world till ye find,
　(Fog o' th' fen and salt o' th' sea)
　　Now quick and now slow.
　　Above and below,
　　Away let us go !
Where he is buried lay me.

Gone is the sweet o' th' rose,
　(Fog o' th' fen and salt o' th' sea)

Where it is he only knows,
   (Fog o' th' fen and salt o' th' sea)
     The skies are not blue,
     Nor sparkles the dew,
     All hearts are untrue—
   Naught but the salt o' th' sea !

CHARLES LOTIN HILDRETH.

THE FACE OF LOVE.

BUT once beheld by any man, no more ;
   And then with such wild tumult in his
     brain
He may not recollect the look it wore,
   Or if 't was pleasure that he felt, or pain,
When those strange eyes sent fire to his heart's
     core.

But who can grasp the maze of sad delight
   That music weaves, its memory dying never?
And who can read the face of love aright,
   With all its mystic meanings, shifting ever,
That stir life's deepest springs, yet cheat the
     sight?

A face of godlike glory, such as men
  Might well misdeem the majesty of heaven,
But that there ever comes and goes again—
  Like clouds across the noonday brilliance
      driven—
A mien that makes it wholly human then.

Full-lipped as Orient maidens, there may play
  The dimpled meaning that has shaken thrones
And swept a nation's boundaries away,
  And then a quiver, as of voiceless groans,
And all the face looks tragic, old, and gray.

At times a sad, mysterious face, that seems
  With startled eyes to watch for coming ill;
Yet ever and anon across it gleams
  A smile, that, passing, leaves it cold and still,
Enwrapped in unimaginable dreams.

LOVE.

LOVE was primeval; from forgotten time
  Come hints of common lives by love made
      great,
In pastoral song or fragmentary rhyme,
  While fades the fame of many a warlike state.
Love lives forever though we pass away;
  Still shall there be hot hearts and longing
      eyes,

Hyperion youths and maids more fair than they,
  Loath lips and lingering hands and parting
     sighs,
When we have vanished, and our simple doom
  Is blended with the themes of old romance,
Ay, from our dust young buds and flowers shall
    bloom,
  To deck bright tresses in the spring-tide dance,
And be the mute, sweet signs of love confessed
  To Passioned hopes upon a maiden's breast.

RICHARD EDWIN DAY.

SAPPHIRES.

MY love has neither gold nor gems
  Save that she wears in modest wise,
Bluer than flash in diadems,
  Two sapphires like the midnight skies.

Afar in their pellucid deeps
  Are stars that quickly rise and set ;
And each a mystic meaning keeps
  Which no astrology may get.

Shy opals not so liquid gleam
  As the soft sapphires of my love ;

And oft I fancy that they dream
Of what her heart is dreaming of.

Before, what mortal ever knew
Twin gems that held the wearer's soul,
While in and out, amid their hue,
Her spirit's sweetest passions stole?

GOLD.

FORTUNE, weird dame, shakes the uncanny
gold
With awkward favor from her jingling horn,
Not so the soncy fay whose fingers told
Out all the wealth of cowslips and of corn,
And all that wings of yellow finches hold.

There is more craft in her light, sunny toil
Than in the hands that shape the gold of Ind.
They could not hide a jewel in the coil
Of budded lilies, rocking in the wind,
Or tinge the petals with so dainty foil.

But she enriches in more cunning wise
The cat-tails keeping in their rough brown
nap
A glint of gold, and subtler treasure lies
In the centre of the dandelion's cap,
And in the silken hood the maize unties.

Yet all her lesser work is but despair ;
  For once she made a woman's locks of brown,
And strewed a glittering treasure in her hair,
  Ah ! wily mesh, and strong beyond renown !
The sunshine and my heart are in the snare.

CLINTON SCOLLARD.

O LADY MINE.

O LADY mine, with the sunlit hair,
  The birds are carolling blithe and gay
In the bourgeoning boughs that sway the air
  O'er the grassy aisles of the orchard way.
  The mock-bird pipes to the busy jay :
There 's a gleam of white on the vines that twine
  Where your casement opes to the golden day,
    O lady mine !

O lady mine, with the sunlit hair,
  The rills are glad that the month is May ;
The dawns are bright and the eves are fair
  O'er the grassy aisles of the orchard way.
  The dales have doffed their robes of gray,
The bending buttercups spill their wine,
  There is joy in the heart of faun and fay,
    O lady mine !

O lady mine, with the sunlit hair,
  The bees, the ruthless bandits, prey
On the blooms that part their lips in prayer,
  O'er the grassy aisles of the orchard way,
  From the evening shores where the nereids
      play,
The breezes blow o'er the foamy brine,
  And I dream I hear them softly say,
      " O lady mine ? "

Envoy.

O lady mine, wilt thou not stray
O'er the grassy aisles of the orchard way,
And list to Love where the wind-flowers play,
      O lady mine !

ACROSS THE CRIMSON CLOVER SEAS.

ACROSS the crimson clover seas,
  I hear the haunting hum of bees,
That rifled all the rich perfume
From jasmine and magnolia bloom,
When, with his pallid, icy hands,
Chill winter bound our northern lands ;
To spicy, palm-embowered isles,
Where never-dying summer smiles,
My spirit drifts upon the breeze,
Across the crimson clover seas.

And where the gulf-stream softly laves
Floridian capes with foamy waves,
I see the bearded cypress boughs,
Like hoary hermits, lift their brows
Aloft to greet a sky as clear
As any placid mountain mere ;
And there the merry mocking-birds
Seem uttering melodious words ;
How soon the golden vision flees
Across the crimson clover seas !

The vision fades.   Ah ! well it may,
For one who makes more bright the day
Down greening aisles of tall grass trips,
A song upon her lovely lips,
As merry as the thrush above,
Out-trilling tuneful lays of love ;
And all my pulses swifter stir,
And all my heart goes out to her,
The while she strays in graceful ease
Across the crimson clover seas.

FRANK DEMPSTER SHERMAN.

A MADRIGAL.

SWEETHEART, the year is young,
   And 'neath the heavens blue
The fresh wild-flowers have hung
   Their cups to catch the dew.
And love like a bird carols one soft word,
   Sweetheart, to the sapphire skies;
And floating aloft comes an echo soft
   "Sweetheart"—your eyes!

Sweetheart, the year is sweet
   With fragrance of the rose
That bends before your feet
   As to the gale that blows.
And love like a bird quavers one low word,
   Sweetheart, to the garden place;
And across the glow comes an echo low
   "Sweetheart"—your face!

Sweetheart, the year grows old,
   Upon the meadows brown,
And forests, waving gold,
   The stars look, trembling, down.

And love like a bird whispers one pure word,
   Sweetheart, to the cooling air ;
And the breezes sure waft an echo pure
   " Sweetheart "—your hair !

Sweetheart, the year wanes fast ;
   The summer birds have flown
From winter's spiteful blast
   Unto a sun-bound zone.
And love like a bird warbles one clear word,
   Sweetheart, to the balmy south ;
And back to my ear comes an echo clear
   "Sweetheart "—your mouth !

Sweetheart, the year is gone ;
   Lean closer to my heart !
Time only weighs upon
   The loves that dwell apart.
And love like a bird with his whole soul stirred,
   Sweetheart, shall carol his glee ;
And to you I 'll cling while the echoes ring
   "Sweetheart "—for me !

AWAKE, AWAKE.

AWAKE, awake, O gracious heart—
   There 's some one knocking at the door :
The chilling breezes make him smart ;
   His little feet are tired and sore.
16

Arise, and welcome him before
    Adown his cheeks the big tears start :
Awake, awake, O gracious heart
    There 's some one knocking at the door.

'T is Cupid come with loving art
    To honor, worship, and implore ;
And lest, unwelcomed, he depart
    With all his wise mysterious lore,
Awake, awake, O gracious heart,
    There 's some one knocking at the door.

CHARLES G. D. ROBERTS.

DARK.

NOW, for the night is hushed and blind with
     rain,
  My soul desires communion, Dear, with thee,
  But hour by hour my spirit gets not free,—
Hour by still hour my longing strives in vain,
The thick dark hems me, ev'n to the restless
     brain,
  The wind's confusion vague encumbers me,
  Ev'n passionate memory, grown too faint to
     see
Thy features, stirs not in her straitening chain.

And thou, dost thou too feel this strange divorce
  Of will from power? The spell of night and
      wind,
Baffling desire and dream, dost thou too find ?
Not distance parts us, Dear ; but this dim force,
  Intangible, holds us helpless, hushed with
      pain,
Dumb with the dark, blind with the gusts of
      rain !

RONDEAU.

WITHOUT one kiss she 's gone away
    And stol'n the brightness out of day ;
  With scornful lips and haughty brow
  She 's left me melancholy now,
In spite of all that I could say.

And so, to guess as best I may
What angered her, a while I stay
    Beneath this blown acacia bough
    Without one kiss ;

Yet all my wildered brain can pay
My questioning, is but to pray
    Persuasion may my speech endow,
    And Love may never more allow
My injured sweet to sail away
    Without one kiss.

ELLA HIGGINSON.

ONE KISS.

IF we, who never met, should **meet,**
  And, after meeting, come to know
That if we had but sooner met
  We might have loved each other so ;

If, after meeting many times,
  The thought should swell into regret
That God had not ordained it **so,**
  That we in freedom could have met ;

If, looking in each other's eyes—
  The while both knew the same sweet care,
And all but passion—conquered—we
  Should read the same thought written there ;

If, knowing, then, that we must walk
  Henceforth in ways as far apart
As sea to sea, because each saw
  What trembled in the other's heart ;

Then, if for but one single time,
  Well knowing, too, that it was wrong,
Our lips should meet in one last kiss,
  Replete with passion, tender, long ;

Would this, I say, be sin so black—
  Let those all-sinless cast the stone—
’That a whole blameless after-life
  Could never for it quite atone?

THE ANGEL IN HELL.

THE Devil he stood at the gates of Hell
  And yearned for an angel above,
And he sighed:—“Come down, sweet siren,
  and learn
The lesson **of** passion and love!”

The angel she leaned from the gates of gold,
  (The Devil was fair **in** her eyes,)
And she thought it would be very nice if she
  Could lift him up to the skies.

“**My** dear Mr. **Devil,**” she softly replied:
  “**My home is of** comfort and ease,
And I ’m very **well** satisfied where I am—
  And so—if you ’ll pardon me—please,

“ I hardly dare **venture** to go so far:
  Do you, sir, come up **to me,**
For I am an angel in heaven, while you
  Are only the Devil, you see.”

"Too well I know that an angel you are,"
  The Devil with cunning replied:
" And that is the reason I covet you
  For a safe-guard at my side.

"You 'll find the atmosphere balmy and **warm,**
  And a heart that is wholly thine,
Here are red, red roses, and passionate bliss,
  And kisses, and maddening wine.

"O, come! angel, come! I 'll stretch **out** my
    arms,
  And draw you to infinite rest,
And all the delights of this beautiful hell,
  Asleep, you shall drink on my breast!"

The angel she leaned from the gates of gold
  And she clasped him with arms of snow:
But the while she was striving to draw him up,
  The lower she seemed to go.

" Don't struggle, sweet angel," the Devil he
    cried,
  As he bore her on passion's swell:
" When an angel's arms have embraced me but
    once,
  She belongs to the Devil—and hell."

ANNE REEVES ALDRICH.

THE END.

DO you recall that little room
　　Close blinded from the searching sun,
So dim, my blossoms dreamed of dusk ;
　　And shut their petals one by one ?
—And then a certain crimson eve,
　　The death of day upon the tide ;
How all its blood spread on the waves,
　　And stained its waters far and wide.
　　　　　Ah, you forget ;
　　　　　But I remember yet.

When I awake in middle night,
　　And stretch warm hands to touch your face,
There is no chance that I shall find
　　Aught but your chill and empty place.
I have no bitter word to say,
　　The Past is worth this anguish sore,
—But mouth to mouth, and heart to heart,
　　No more on earth, O God, no more !
　　　　　For Love is dead,
　　　　　Would 't were I, instead.

DREAMS.

So still I lay within his arms
   He dreamed I was asleep,
Across my lips I felt his breath
   Like burning breezes creep.
I felt his watchful, searching gaze,
   Though closed eyes cannot see ;
I felt his warm and tender grasp
   More closely prison me.

The waking dream was all too sweet
   For me to wish to sleep.
I was too far beyond Earth's woes
   To speak, or smile, or weep.
How after this, could I endure
   The troublous times of Age and Tears,
To sit and wait for Death to dawn
   Across the midnight of my years !

Love will not stay, though we entreat ;
   Death will not come at call.
Ah, to return to life and grief !
   Ah, having risen, to fall !
I felt his mouth burn on my own ;
   I raised my eyes to his eyes' deep.
He thought his kiss had wakened me,
   He dreamed I was asleep.

AN AWAKENING.

LOVE had forgotten and gone to sleep ;
    Love had forgotten the present and past.
I was so glad when he ceased to weep,
    "Now he is quiet," I whispered, "at last."

What sent you here on that night of all nights,
    Breaking his slumber, dreamless and deep?
Just as I whispered below my breath :
    "Love has forgotten and gone to sleep."

AMÉLIE RIVES-CHANLER.

LOVE SONG.

THE moon shines pale in the Western sky,
    Like a pearl set over a brow that blushes,
There is many a homeward bird in the air,
    And the hedges thrill with the thrushes.

Though my love be further away from me
    Than the East from the West, or the Day
        from the Night,
I have turned my face to his dwelling-place,
    And I bid him "Good-night," "good-night."

Though he less can feel my hurrying breath
  Than the tree the bird that lilts on its bough,
Yet since the winds Love's messengers be,
  They will bear him my kisses, I trow ! —

O moon ! shine first on my lips and then
  Go shine on the forehead of him I love !
He will dream perchance that an angel's wing
  Has quivered his brow above ! —

And sing, ye birds, in his ears the song
  My heart is singing within my breast ;
It will thrill his heartstrings with ecstasy,
  And possess his soul with rest.

Ye, **too, O** fragrance of earth and flower,
  And voices of night in May !
Watch near him until in the Eastern field
  Blossom the roses of day.

But thou, O wind ! lay close on his lips
  The kisses thou hast in thy flight,
And he will stir in his sleep, and wake,
  And whisper — " My heart — good-night."

WHY?

HEART of me, why do you sigh ?
  Why droop your eyelids, pale and **shy,**
Like snow-flakes that on violets lie ? —
  Why do you sigh, **my heart?**

Sweeting, wherefore do you weep? —
'Til the flowers that May winds steep,
When the day hath sunk to sleep,
Seem from beads o' dew to peep ! —
     Why do you weep, my sweet?

O my love, whence comes this glow,
Like the sunset on the snow,
Which on your fair face doth show ? —
     Why do you blush, my queen ?

Must I speak your answer, dear ?
Listen then, and you will hear
Why you sigh and weep and blush,
Why e'en now you bid me hush :
Sing, O sing, ye birds that be ;
Answer, music of the sea ;
Spin, old earth, to melody ; —
For my one love loveth me —
     Does she not, my heart ?

LOVE'S GHOST.

THE wan moon luiks fu' patiently
   From oot a scarf o' rainbow licht,
Like a woman pale wi' mony a grief
   Drest oot in colors bricht.

The stars are eyes, sad, sad wi' tears,
   The clouds are faëry winding-sheets,

The trees grim han's reached up in prayer,
  An' the wind a ghaist that greets.

Anither ghaist gangs at my side,
  Wi' eyes like stars, sad, sad wi' tears,
His wastit han's reach up in prayer,
  His sobs torment my ears.

Pale ghaist o' luve, gang on, gang on ;
  Why will ye ever haunt me sae?
Ye are a part o' hours fled,
  A piece o' yesterday.

I know ye not.   Flit, flit awa' ;
  Your eyes like fires burn in my heart.
Wraith o' fause luve, haunt not the leal ;—
  In true luve's name, depart.

JESSIE F. O'DONNELL.

A VALENTINE.

HAVE you counted **the** thistle's **wandering**
      flakes
  That the wind scatters lightly round him?
Or the plumes that the gray **old** dandelion
      shakes
  From the feathery wreath that crowned him?

Do you know how often the daisies
  Have tempted the wind to woo?
Or the rose has blushed at his praises?—
  Then number my thoughts of you.

Can you measure a bluebird's quivering flight?
  Or the speed of a homesick swallow,
When the sunbeams have fled far south in the
      night,
  And the birds and the wild bees follow?
Do you think while watching them winging
  So fast down their pathway blue,
That my thoughts as swiftly are swinging
  World-over to follow you?

Have you looked in the violets' innocent eyes?
  Have the lilies breathed once o'er you?
Have they opened their fragrant hearts to the
      skies,
And kissed the June breezes before you?
Have you heard the voices of showers
  Go murmuring all night through
A rhythm of love to the flowers?—
  So sweet are my thoughts of you.

Have you watched the blooms by zephyrs be-
      guiled
  From the apple-trees gently stealing?
Have you seen o'er the weary eyes of a child
  The lashes drop slumberous healing?

Do you know how soft the caresses
From lips of the gracious dew
That fall on the blossoms he blesses?—
So tender my thoughts of you.

You remember how surely violets will greet
The first steps of the joyous summer,
And you know how the daisies spring **round**
the feet
Of the radiant, welcome comer.
The ripe fruit brings gold to September,
And roses to June are true,
And my thoughts, beloved, remember,
Are faithful as these to you.

SONG FROM "HENDRIK HUDSON."

MY beloved! My beloved!
In my dreams I heard sweet voices
Singing, saying, that a stranger
Should sail up the mighty river,
Sent by Manitou, the giver;
When the birch in gold rejoices,
When **the** tricksy frost-sprites change her
Leaflets green to garments yellow,
Steeped in sunshine warm and mellow,
My beloved! My beloved!

My beloved! My beloved!
Long I waited for thy coming,

As the earth awaits the showers,
List'ning ever, thirsty, yearning,
For thy footsteps toward me turning:
Heard them in the partridge's drumming,
Felt thy sweet breath from the flowers,
Heard thy voice through woodlands ringing
In the bluebird's joyous singing;
  My beloved! My beloved!

My beloved! My beloved!
As the lilies, snowy, slender,
Lift their cups for dewy blessing,
So I lift my heart's white flower
For thy love's refreshing shower.
Clasp me in thy arms so tender,
Thrill me with thy lips' caressing,
Fervent as the West-Wind woo me,
All my soul lies open to thee:
  My beloved! My beloved!

INTO THE DARK.

I GAZE into the dark, O Love!
  I gaze into the dark,
The creeping shadows chill me; and the Night,
  With wide-outreaching arms, holds thee afar.
O yearning eyes! Your love, 'midst wondrous
    light
  More fair than falls from moon-ray or from star,
    Smiles out into the dark.

I reach into the dark, O Love!
  I reach into the dark.
I cannot find thee; and my groping hands
  Touch only memories and phantom shapes.
O empty arms! Be glad of those sweet lands
  Wherein your love all loneliness escapes,
     And smiles into the dark.

I call into the dark, O Love!
  I call into the dark.
There comes from out the hush below, above,
  No answer but my own quick-fluttered breath.
O doubting heart! Dost thou not know **thy**
    love,
  Across the awful silentness of death,
Smiles at thee through the dark?

LIZETTE WOODWORTH REESE.

A THOUGHT OF MAY.

ALL that long, mad March day in **the dull
  town,**
  I had a thought of May—alas! alas!
The dogwood boughs made whiteness up and
    down;

The daffodils were burning in the grass :
And there were bees astir in lane and street,
  And scent of lilacs blowing tall and lush ;
While hey, the wind, that pitched its voice so
      sweet,
  It seemed an angel talked behind each bush !
The west grew very golden, roofs turned black.
  I saw one star above the gables bare,
The door flew open. Love, you had come back.
  I held my arms ; you found the old way there.
In its old place you laid your yellow head,
And at your kiss the mad March weather fled.

BETRAYED.

SHE is false, O Death, she is fair !
    Let me hide my head on thy knee,
Blind mine eyes, dull mine ears, O Death !
    She hath broke my heart for me !

Give me a perfect dream ;
    Find me a rare, dim place ;
But let not her voice come nigh,
    And keep out her face—her face !
      17

L. BLANCHE FEARING.

WHERE ART THOU, DARLING?

WHERE art thou, darling? **Dost thou lean**
   Thy forehead from yon silver star?
While in the ether ocean vast
Titanic suns go sweeping past
Like ships with shrouds of fire? Dost ween
How I do stand and weep afar?

Hast thou forgot **the** mighty **love**
With which I circled thee below?
Do bright-haired angels, folding thee
With their white pinions tenderly,
Salute thee in thy rest above
With deeper love than I could show?

As round a sun pale planets burn
In bright-revolving clusters, **so**
Around thy forehead, precious one,
Which was my life, my light, my sun,
All hopes and purposes did turn,
Circle **and cluster,** change and glow.

Where art thou, darling? I entreat
Of sages, and they answer **me :**

"Beyond the purlieus of all time,
In sempiternal spheres sublime
Which lie at rest about God's feet,
Somewhere he lives eternally."

O blind abstraction! Here I reel,
And clutch the air, and strive for breath!
Oh, Somewhere is too near akin
To Nowhere for my soul to win
A gleam of hope which back might feel
Through the black gallery of death!

*   *   *   *   *   *

Ah, Somewhere out there in the night!—
Mad am I, that I know not where!—
Somewhere, Somewhere!—O God, be just!
Remember that I am but dust!
Strengthen mine eyelids for the light
Of thy great mysteries laid bare!

*   *   *   *   *   *

Where art thou, darling? Lo! I hold
My poor face to the dumb gray sky;
The downy pinions of the snow
Strike soft against it as they go:
Come, darling, on my forehead cold
Lay thy soft finger-tips, and I

Shall be content a little while ;
For though upon my death-numb brow
Thy hand fell lighter than the snow,
My darling, I should surely know
That it were thine, and **I** could smile,—
A grace I have forgotten now.

Where art thou, darling ?   Like a bell
Ringing most sweetly down the broad
Abyss which gaps 'twixt Heaven and Time,
I hear thy voice : **a** sweeter chime
It taketh on, a loftier swell ;
It whispers, " Love, Somewhere with God ! "

Oh, sweeter than the tuneful wave
That creeps up singing from the sea,
Sweeter than Hermes' chorded shell,
Oh, richer than deep organ swell
Through echoing transept, aisle, and nave,—
" Somewhere with God I wait for thee ! "

FROM " HUMAN LOVE'S WEAKNESS."

OH ! human love doth underrun
    And overrun all human things ;
When it is crushed, life reels and swounds,
And gaspeth from a hundred wounds ;
Earth staggers ; darkness blinds the sun
As with a multitude of wings.

Love spins her magical cocoon
About our souls,—and that 's our world.
We think the earth rocks when we shake ;
We think the stars clash when we break,
On some still, stormless night in June,
From Love's frail leaf about us curled.

MISCELLANEOUS

MISCELLANEOUS

WHEN THE PALE MOON.

WHEN the pale, pale moon arose last night,
  Its cold light fell on my silent floor,
And I thought of a face so pure and white,
  That vanished in years that will come no
    more !
O pale, sweet face—sweet face ! I said,
  Come sit by the window still as of yore,
O pale, sweet face, so dear—and dead !—
  Come look from the moon on my silent floor.

And a voice I heard—oh, sweet and dear !—
  That hushed the stir of the rustling bough,
From my window in heaven I lean, I hear,
  The moonlight I see on thy pale, pale brow—
O pale, sweet face,—sweet face ! I said,

Come sit by the window evermore
Look down, dear eyes, so long, long fled,
   Come look from the moon on my silent floor,
Silent, silent, forevermore!

John Hugh McNaughton.

WE TWO.

Ah, painful sweet! how can I take it in!
    That somewhere in the illimitable blue
  Of God's pure space, which men call Heaven,
      we two
Again shall find each other, and begin
The infinite life of love, a life akin
    To angels,—only angels never knew
    The ecstasy of blessedness that drew
Us to each other, even in this world of sin.

Yea, find each other! the remotest star
    Of all the galaxies would hold in vain
Our souls apart, that have been heretofore
    As closely interchangeable as are
One mind and spirit.   Oh, joy! **that aches to**
      pain,
To be together—we two—forevermore!

Margaret J. Preston.

THREE KISSES OF FAREWELL.

THREE, only three, my darling,
  Separate, solemn, slow;
Not like the swift and joyous ones
  We used to know
When we kissed because we loved each other
  Simply to taste love's sweet,
And lavished our kisses as the summer
  Lavishes heat.
But as they kiss whose hearts are wrung,
  When hope and fear are spent,
And nothing left to give, except
  A sacrament!

First of the three, my darling,
  Is sacred unto pain;
We have hurt each other often;
  We shall again,
When we pine because we miss each other,
  And do not understand
How the written words are so much colder
  Than eye and hand.
I kiss thee, dear, for all such pain
  Which we may give or take;
Buried, forgiven before it comes
  For our love's sake!

The second kiss, my darling,
  Is full of joy's sweet thrill ;
We have blessed each other always ;
  We always will.
We shall reach until we feel each other,
  Past all of time and space ;
We shall listen till we hear each other
  In every place ;
The earth is full of messengers,
  Which love sends to and fro ;
I kiss thee, darling, for all joy
  Which we shall know.

The last kiss, oh, my darling,
  My love—I cannot see
Through my tears, as I remember
  What it may be.
We may die and never see each other,
  Die with no time to give
Any signs that our hearts are faithful
  To die **as** live.
Token of what they will not see
  Who see our parting breath,
This one last kiss, my darling, seals
  The seal of death !

"Saxe Holm."

CREED.

I BELIEVE if I should die,
    And you should kiss my eyelids when I lie
Cold, dead and dumb to all this world con-
        tains,
The folded orbs would open at thy breath,
And from its exile in the isles of death,
    Life would come gladly back along my veins.

I believe if I were dead,
And you upon my lifeless heart should tread,
    Not knowing what the poor clod chanced to
        be,
It would find sudden pulse beneath the touch
Of him it ever loved in life so much,
    And throb again, warm, tender, true to thee.

I believe if on my grave,
Hidden in woody deeps or by the wave,
    Your eyes should drop some warm tears of
        regret,
From every salty seed of your dear grief
Some fair, sweet blossom would leap into leaf,
    To prove death could not make my love for-
        get.

I believe if I should fade
Into those mystic realms where light is **made**
  And you should long once more my face to see
I would come forth upon the hills of night
And gather stars, like fagots, till thy sight,
  Led by their beacon-blaze, fell full on me!

I believe my faith in thee,
Strong as my life, so nobly placed to be,
  I would as soon expect to see the sun
Fall like a dead king from his height sublime,
His glory stricken from the throne of time,
  As thee unworth the worship thou hast **won**.

I believe who hath not loved,
Hath half the sweetness of his life unproved;
  Like one, who with the grape within his
     grasp,
Drops it with all its crimson juice unpressed,
And all its luscious sweetness left unguessed,
  Out from his careless and unheeding clasp.

I believe love, pure and true,
Is to the soul a sweet, immortal dew
  That gems life's petals in its hours of **dusk—**
The waiting angels see and recognize
The rich crown-jewel, love, **of** Paradise,
  When life falls from us like a withered husk.

              Mary Ashley Townsend.

JIMMY'S WOOING.

THE wind came blowing out of the West,
  As Jimmy mowed the hay ;
The wind came blowing out of the West ;
It stirred the beech tree out of rest,
And rocked the bluebird up in his nest,
  As Jimmy mowed the hay.

The swallows skimmed along the ground,
  As Jimmy mowed the hay ;
The swallows skimmed along the ground,
And rustling leaves made a pleasant sound,
Like children babbling all around,
  As Jimmy mowed the hay.

Milly came with her bucket by,
  As Jimmy mowed the hay ;
Milly came with her bucket by,
With wee light foot so trim and sly,
And sunburnt cheek and laughing eye,
  As Jimmy mowed the hay.

A rustic Ruth in linsey gown ;—
  And Jimmy mowed the hay ;
A rustic Ruth in linsey gown,
He watched the soft cheeks' changing brown,

And the long dark lash that trembled **down**
  Whenever he looked that way.

And Milly's heart was good as **gold,**
  As Jimmy mowed the hay ;
Oh Milly's heart was good as gold,
But Jimmy thought her shy and cold,
And more than that he had never told,
  As Jimmy mowed the hay.

The wind came gathering up his bands,
  As Jimmy mowed the hay ;
The wind came gathering up his bands,
With the cloud and the lightning in his hands
And a shadow darkening all the lands,
  As Jimmy mowed **the** hay.

The rain came pattering down amain,
  Where Jimmy mowed the hay ;
The rain came pattering down amain,
And **under a** thatch of the laden wain,
Jimmy and Milly, a cosy twain,
  Sat sheltered by the hay.

For Milly nestled to Jimmy's breast,
  Under the thatch of hay ;
For Milly nestled to Jimmy's breast ;
A wild bird fluttering home to nest,

And then, I swear she looked her best
  Under the thatch of hay.

And when the sun came laughing out,
  Over the ruined hay ;
And when the sun came laughing out,
Milly had ceased to pet and pout,
And twittering birds began to shout
  As if for a Wedding Day.

Will Wallace Harney.

THE FLIGHT FROM THE CONVENT.

I SEE the star-lights quiver
  Like jewels in the river ;
The bank is hid with sedge ;
What if I slip the edge ?
  I thought I knew the way
  By night as well as day.
How soon a lover goes astray !

The place is somewhat **lonely**—
I mean, **for** just one only,
I brought the boat ashore
An hour ago, or more.
  Well, I will sit and wait ;
  She fixed the **hour** at eight.
Good angels ! bring her not too late !

To-morrow's tongues that name her
Will hardly dare to blame her;
A lily still is white
Through all the dark of night;
　　The morning sun shall show
　　A bride as pure as snow,
Whose wedding all the world shall know.

O God! that I should gain her!
But what can so detain her?
Hist! yelping cur! that bark
Will fright her in the dark.
　　What! striking nine! that 's fast!
　　Was some one walking past?
Oho! **so** thou art come at last!

Now, why thy long delaying?
Alack! thy beads and praying!
If thou, a saint, dost hope
To kneel and kiss the Pope,
　　Then I, a sinner, know
　　Where sweeter kisses grow—
Nay, now, just once before we go!

Nay, twice, and by Saint Peter,
The second was the sweeter!
Quickly now, and in the boat,
Good-by, old tower and moat!
　　May mildew from the sky

  Drop blindness on the eye
That looks to watch as you go by!

O saintly maid! I told thee
No convent walls should hold thee,
Look! yonder comes the moon!
We started not too soon,
  See how we pass the mill!
  What! is the night too chill?
Then **I** must fold thee closer still!

Theodore Tilton.

SUMMER LOVE.

I KNOW 't is late but let me stay,
 For night is tenderer than day;
Sweet love, dear love, I cannot go;
Dear love, sweet love, I love thee so.
The birds are in the grove asleep,
The katydids shrill concert keep,
The woodbine breathes a fragrance rare,
To please the dewy, languid air,
The fire-flies twinkle in the vale,
The river shines in moonlight pale.
See yon bright star! choose it for thine,
And call its near companion mine;
Yon air-spun lace above the moon,—
'T will veil her radiant beauty soon;

And look ! a meteor's dreamy light
Streams mystic through the solemn night.
Ah, life glides swift, like that still fire,
How soon our gleams of joy expire.
Who can be sure the present kiss
Is not the last?   Make all of this.
I know 't is late, dear love, I know,
Dear love, sweet love, I love thee so.

It cannot be the stealthy day
That turns the orient darkness gray ;
Heardst thou? I thought or feared I heard
Vague twitters of some wakeful bird.
Nay, 't was but summer in her sleep
Low murmuring from the leafy deep,
Fantastic mist obscurely fills
The hollows of Kentucky hills.
The wings of night are swift indeed !
Why makes the jealous morn such speed?
This rose thou wear'st may I not take
For passionate remembrance' sake ?
Press with thy lips its crimson heart,
Yes, blushing rose, we must depart.
A rose cannot return a kiss—
I pay its due with this, and this.
The stars grow faint, they soon will **die,**
But love fades not, nor fails.   Good-by !
Unhappy joy—delicious pain—
We part, in love, we meet again.

Good-by !—the morning dawns—I go ;
Dear love, sweet love, I love thee so.

William Henry Venable.

CAPTURED.

NANETTE !
    Can you not teach me **to** forget ?
It is **so** hard to understand !
You would not lift your slender hand
To keep me yours ; yet must I be
Yours, only yours, eternally.
Though 'neath the chain I strive and fret,
Nanette !

That golden hour when first we met,
Like the swift inundating sea
Love's tide swept in and conquered me.
A moment you were touched and stirred ;
Ah, that 's the anguish of regret,
Nanette !

My every thought on you was set,
I poured for you love's priceless wine,
You could no more its power divine
Than one small blossom's cup of gold
The boundless firmament could hold ;
My eyes with scornful tears are wet,
Nanette !

This withered spray of mignonette
You gave me, from my heart I take,
This sick sad heart you taught to ache,
And fling it in the restless sea—
I would my thoughts of you could be
So flung away from me ; and yet,
Nanette !

I cannot break the cruel net,
Though I may curse my fate and swear
You are not kind, nor good nor fair,
You 'll hold me by one silken tress,
Or eyelids' down-dropped loveliness,
A touch of hand, or tone of voice,
Or smile that all my will destroys ;
Ah, heaven ! the only boon I crave
Is rest, the silence of the grave.
Release me ! teach me to forget,
Nanette !

Celia Thaxter.

WHAT THE WOLF REALLY SAID TO LITTLE RED-RIDING-HOOD.

WONDERING maiden, so puzzled and fair,
    Why dost thou murmur and ponder and
        stare ?
" Why are thy eyelids so open and wild ? "
Only the better to see with, my child !
Only the better and clearer to view
Cheeks that are rosy, and eyes that are blue.

Dost thou still wonder, and ask why these arms
Fill thy soft bosom with tender alarms?
Swaying so wickedly—are they misplaced,
Clasping or shielding some delicate waist?
Hands whose coarse sinews may fill you with fear
Only the better protect you, my dear!

Little Red Riding-Hood, when in the street
Why do I press your small hand when we meet?
Why when you timidly offered your cheek,
Why did I sigh, and why did n't I speak?
Why, well, you see—if the truth must appear—
I 'm not your grandmother, Riding-Hood, Dear!

Francis Bret Harte.

SONG.

LIKE a fettered boat that pants and pulls,
   And struggles to be free,
When the wind is up, and the whirling gulls
   Are wild with ecstasy—
   Is my heart apart from thee!

Like a boat that leans, that leaps, that flies,
   That sings along the sea,
With a sunny shower of drops that rise
   And fall melodiously—
   Is my heart, sweetheart, is my heart,
   Is my heart approaching thee!

Robert Kelley Weeks.

LOVE'S RETURN.

THOU art as welcome as the summer rain
   To thirsty rootlets that, beneath the sod,
  Await its call to turn the rusty clod
To one wide, waving field of happy grain !
Thou art as welcome as rest after pain,—
   As welcome as, when after Sorrow's rod,
  There comes the sweet peace of the loving
     God,—
As welcome as the shore that wrecked men
    gain !

When thou dost go, **the** sunshine leaves the sky,
  And all the life seems vanished from the air,
   And vain seem all the gains and hopes of
    men.
But when, once more, I know thy coming nigh,
  The sun breaks out and all the earth is fair,
   And every thing bursts into song again !

Minot J. Savage.

REGRET.

NOW, that you come no more to me,
   O love, how dreary life has grown !
There is no song of bird or bee
   That for your silence can atone ;
   And since **I** go my ways alone,
There is no light on land **or sea.**

The fragrant messengers of June—
    White jessamine and brier-rose—
Breathe through the golden afternoon
    On every wind **that comes** and **goes :**
    I care for no sweet breath that blows,
The whole world **being out of** tune.

What is an idle word to make
    Such shadow where was sun **before ?**
When **others sleep,** I watch **and** wake,
    And restless pace my chamber-floor :
    Now, that you come **to** me **no** more,
O love, it seems my heart **must** break.

And these are days !   How shall it be
    If years must drag the lengthening chain
Of sad and bitter memory ?
    How shall we live our lives again,
    With all its sweetness spent in vain ?
O love, come back once more to me !

Mary Elizabeth Blake.

SI, DO, RE.

SHE 's only a singin' a tune that he taught
        'er,
Is Evelyn Lee, the poor dairyman's daughter.
Who taught 'er ? you ask. Why ! the singin'
        school **master,**

Who always smiled sweetly whenever he passed
    her,
And made her heart beat just a wee bit the
    faster.
  They say that she loves him; be that as it
    may,
  Let her sing if she wants to! Sol, fa, me, si,
    do, re!

The singin' school closed when the evenin's
    grew shorter,
But still she keeps singin', the dairyman's
    daughter.
She goes to her task with the first peep o' day,
And whatever her thoughts may be, keeps
    singin' away—
While changin' the milk into cheese, curd, and
    whey.
  They say that she's lonesome; be that as it
    may,
  Let her sing if she wants to! Sol, fa, me, si,
    do, re!

Where's the master, I wonder? He's gone, I
    suppose.
He has n't? What keeps him? Look, look!
    there he goes!
And sure as I live, there's the dairyman's
    daughter,
A saunterin' out for a pail o' fresh water,

She sees him, and runs for the house, but he 's
        caught her
    And kissed her—and she—well, be that as **it**
        may,
    They 'll be married to-day, so they say.
    To-day? You don't say ! Sol, fa, me, si, do, re **!**

Mrs. B. C. Rude.

A WOMAN'S GIFTS.

FIRST, I would give thee—nay, I may and
        will—
Thoughts, memory, prayers, a sacred wealth
        unguessed,
My soul's own glad and beautiful bequest,
Conveyed in voiceless reverence, deep and still,
As angels give their thoughts and prayers to
    God !
Next, I would yield, in service freely made,
All of my days and years thy needs to fill ;
To bear, or heavy cross, or thorny rod,
Glad of my bondage, deeming it most meet—
A mystery of love, as strange as sweet,
That love from its own wealth should be repaid !
Last, I would give thee, if it pleased thee so,
And for thy pleasure, wishing it increased,
My woman's beauty, heart and lips aglow—
But this, dear, last, **so** soon its charm must fade,
It is, indeed, of all my gifts the least !

Mary Ainge De Vere.

A SONG OF MEETING

OH! passing sweet, my Bird, my Bird,
    Oh! passing sweet!
For thy strain is set to the sweetest word
That ear of an exile ever heard:
    We meet, **we** meet!

Oh! sweet as shelter from the blast,
    Sweet, passing sweet,
The long, long banishment is past—
We meet at last, we meet at last!
    We meet, we meet!

Forceythe Wilson.

CLEOPATRA'S SOLILOQUY.

WHAT care I for the tempest? What care I
    for the rain?
If it beat upon my bosom, would it cool its
    burning pain,—
This pain which ne'er has left me since on his
    heart I lay,
And sobbed my grief at parting as I 'd sob my
    soul away?
O Antony! Antony! **Antony**! When in **thy**
    circling arms

Shall I sacrifice to Eros my glorious woman's
    charms,
And burn life's sweetest incense before his
    sacred shrine,
With the living fire that flashes from thine eyes
    into mine?
Oh, when shall I feel thy kisses rain down
    upon my face,
As a queen of love and beauty, I lie **in thine**
    embrace,
Melting, melting, melting, as a woman only can
When she's a willing captive in the conquering
    arms of man,
As he towers, **a** god above her?—and to yield is
    not defeat,
For love can own no victor if love with love
    shall meet!
I still have regal splendor, I still have queenly
    power,
And more than all, unfaded is woman's glorious
    dower.
But what care I for pleasure? What's beauty
    to me now,
Since Love no longer places his **crown** upon
    my brow?
I have tasted its elixir, its fire has through me
    flashed,
But when the wine glowed brightest, from my
    eager lips 't was dashed.

And I would give all Egypt but once to feel the
    bliss
That thrills through all my being whene'er
    I meet his kiss.
The tempest wildly rages, my hair is wet with
    rain,
But it does not still my longing, or cool my
    burning pain.
For Nature's storms are nothing to the raging
    of my soul
When it burns with jealous frenzy beyond a
    queen's control.
I fear not pale Octavia; that haughty Roman
    dame,
My lion of the desert, my Antony, can tame ;
I fear no Persian beauty, I fear no Grecian maid ;
The world holds not the woman of whom I am
    afraid.
But I 'm jealous of the rapture I tasted in his
    kiss,
And I would not that another should share with
    me that bliss.
No joy would I deny him, let him cull it where
    he will,
So mistress of his bosom is Cleopatra still,—
So that he feels forever, when he Love's nectar
    sips,
'T was sweeter, sweeter, sweeter, **when tasted**
    on my lips ;

So that all other kisses, since he has drawn in
   mine,
Shall **be** unto my lovèd like "water after
   wine."
Awhile let Cæsar fancy Octavia's pallid charms
Can hold Rome's proudest consul a captive
   from these arms.
Her cold embrace but heightens the memory **of**
   mine,
And for my warm caresses he in her arms shall
   pine,
'T was not for love he sought her, but for her
   princely dower ;
She brought him Cæsar's friendship, she
   brought him kingly power,
I should have bid him take her, had he my
   counsel sought,—
I 've but to smile upon him and all her charms
   are naught ;
For I would scorn to hold him by but a single
   hair
Save his own longing for me when I 'm no
   longer there ;
And I will show you, Roman, that for one kiss
   from me,
Wife, fame, and even honor, to him shall nothing be !
Throw wide the window, Isis, fling perfumes
   o'er me now,

And bind the lotus-blossoms again upon my
    brow.
The rain has ceased its weeping, the driving
    storm is past,
And calm are Nature's pulses that lately beat so
    fast.
Gone is my jealous frenzy, and Eros reigns
    serene,
The only god e'er worshipped by Egypt's
    haughty queen.
With Antony, my lovèd, I 'll kneel before his
    shrine,
Till the loves of Mars and Venus are naught
    to his and mine ;
And down through coming ages, in every land
    and tongue,
With them shall Cleopatra and Antony be sung.
Burn sandal-wood and cassia ; let the vapor
    round me wreathe,
And mingle with the incense the lotus-blossoms
    breathe ;
Let India's spicy odors and Persia's perfumes rare
Be wafted on the pinions of Egypt's fragrant air.
With the singing of the night breeze, the river's
    rippling flow,
Let me hear the notes of music in cadence soft
    and low.
Draw round my couch its curtains ; I 'd bathe
    my soul in sleep,

I feel its gentle languor upon me slowly creep.
Oh, let me cheat my senses with dreams of
    future bliss,
In fancy feel his presence, in fancy taste his kiss,
In fancy nestle closely against his throbbing
    heart,
And throw my arms around him, no more, no
    more to part.
Hush! hush! his spirit's pinions are rustling in
    my ears;
He comes upon the tempest to calm my jealous
    fears;
He comes upon the tempest, in answer to my
    call,—
Wife, fame, and even honor, for me he leaves
    them all;
And royally I 'll welcome my lover to my side,
I have won him, I have won him, from Cæsar
    and his bride!

Mary Bayard Clark.

THROUGH THE TREES.

IF I had known whose face I 'd see
    Above the hedge beside the rose;
If I had known whose voice I 'd hear
    Make music where the wind flower blows,—
I had not come; I had not come.

If I had known his deep "I love"
  Could make her face so fair to see;
If I had known her shy "And I"
  Could make him stoop so tenderly,—
I had not come; I had not come.

But what knew I? The summer breeze
  Stopped not to cry "Beware! beware!"
The vine-wreaths dropping from the trees
  Caught not my sleeve with soft "Take care!"
And so I came; and so I came.

The roses that his hands have plucked
  Are sweet to me, are death to me;
Between them, as through living flowers
  I pass, I clutch them, crush them, see!
The bloom for her, the thorn for me.

The brooks leap up with many a song—
  I once could sing, like them could sing;
They fall; 't is like a sigh among
  A world of joy and blossoming.—
Why did I come, why did I come?

The blue sky burns like altar fires—
  How sweet her eyes beneath her hair!
The green earth lights its fragrant pyres,
  The wild birds rise and flush the air;
God looks and smiles, earth is so fair.

But oh ! 'twixt me and you bright heaven,
  Two bending heads pass darkling **by** ;
And loud above the bird and brook,
  I hear a low " I love" " And I,"
And hide my face, Ah, God ! why? why?

Anna Katharine Green Rohlfs.

THE FAIR COPYHOLDER.

YON window frames her like a saint
  Within some old cathedral rare ;
Perhaps she is not quite so quaint,
  And yet I think her full as fair !

All day she scans the written lines,
  Until the last dull proof is ended,
Calling the various words and signs
  By which each error may be mended.

An interceding angel, she,
  'Twixt printing-press and author's pen—
Perhaps she 'd find some faults in me !
  Say, maiden, can you not read *men ?*

Forgive me, gentle girl, but while
  You bravely work I 've been reflecting,
That somewhere in this world of guile,
  There 's some one's life needs **your**
    correcting.

Methinks 't is time you learned this art,
   Which makes the world's wide page read
     better ;
For love needs proving, heart with heart,
   As well as type with written letter.

               Charles H. Crandall.

ALONE.

I MISS you, my darling, my darling,
   The embers burn low on the hearth :
And still is the stir of the household,
   And hushed is the voice of its mirth ;
The rain splashes fast on the terrace,
   The wind past the lattices moans,
The midnight chimes out from the Minster,
   And I am alone.

I want you, my darling, my darling,
   I 'm tired with care and with fret;
I would nestle in silence beside you,
   And all but your presence forget,
In the hush of the happiness given
   To those who through trusting have grown
To the fulness of love in contentment :
   But I am alone.

I call you, my darling, my darling !
  My voice echoes back on the heart ;
I stretch my arms to you in longing,
  And lo ! they fall empty apart ;
I whisper the sweet words you taught me,
  The words that we only have known,
Till the blank of the dumb air is bitter,
  For I am alone.

I need you, my darling, my darling !
  With its yearnings my very heart aches ;
The load that divides us weighs harder ;
  I shrink from the jar that it makes,
Old sorrows rise up to beset me ;
  Old doubts make my spirit their own.
Oh, come through the darkness and save me,
  For I am alone !

Robert J. Burdette.

JACQUEMINOTS.

I MAY not speak in words, dear, but let my
      words be flowers,
  To tell their crimson secret in leaves of crim-
      son fire ;
They plead for smiles and kisses as summer
      fields for showers,
  And every purple veinlet thrills with exquisite
      desire.

O let me see the glance, dear, the glance of soft
    confession
  You give my amorous roses for the tender hope
      they prove ;
And press their sweet leaves back, love, to drink
    their deeper passion,
  For the sweetest, wildest perfume is the
    whisper of my love.

My roses, tell her, pleading all the fondness and
    the sighing
  All the longing of a heart that reaches, thirst-
    ing for its bliss ;
And tell her, tell her, roses, that my lips and
    eyes are dying
  For the melting of her love-look and the rap-
    ture of her kiss.

John Boyle O'Reilly.

ATALANTA.

WHEN spring grows old and sleepy winds
    Set from the south with odors sweet,
I see my love, in green, cool groves,
  Speed down dusk aisles with shining feet.

She throws a kiss and bids me run,
  In whispers sweet as roses' breath ;
I know I cannot win the race,
  And at the end, I know, is death.

But joyfully I bare my limbs,
  Anoint me with the tropic breeze,
And feel through every sinew run
  The vigor of Hippomenes.

O race of love! we all have run
  Thy happy course through groves of spring,
And cared not, when at last we lost,
  For life **or** death or any thing!

                    Maurice P. Thompson.

MY AIN, AIN LASS.

I 'M fain for toys o' Fortune's whyles;
    I ha'e no hate for ranks and styles;
But lairdship o' the braw blue isles
      I 'd e'en let pass
For ane o' her fine tremblin' smiles—
      My ain, ain lass!

I aiblins dream on days to be,
An' feel my heart leap out a wee;
But friendly Fate can grant nae fee
      Could e'en surpass
Her e'en sae dark wi' luve to me—
      My ain, ain lass!

Whyles, gray and ghaistly, by me stand
Auld memories in an eerie band;

But swift as prints on sliding sand
    Sic phantoms pass;
If sae I hauld her warm, warm hand—
    My ain, ain lass!

The past she sweetens through and through,
And, fast as heaven, the future too;
For, surely as her dear soul's due,
    They 'll let me pass!
Wi 'out me there what wad she do,
    My ain, ain lass?

Helen Gray Cone.

FEBRUARY.

NEWLY wedded, and happy quite,
    Careless alike of wind and weather,
Two wee birds from a merry flight,
    Swing in the tree-top, sing together:
Love to them, in the wintry hour,
Summer and sunshine, bud and flower:

So, beloved, when skies are sad,
    Love can render their shadow golden:
A thought of thee, and the day is glad
    As a rose in the dewy dawn unfolden;
And away, away, on passionate wings,
My heart like a bird at thy window sings:

Ina Donna Coolbrith.

A SONG OF FLEETING LOVE.

LOVE has wings as light as a bird,
  Guileless he looks, as a dove, of wrong;
Whatever his song, be it brief or long,
It still has this for an overword:
    Love **has** *wings!*

Though to-day the truant may stay,
  Though he woos and sues and sings,
  Only sorrow to maids he brings;
Pout him and flout him, laugh him **away:**
    Love has wings!

Hold your pulses calm, unstirred—
  Calm and cool as a woodland pool,
  Let not his song your heart befool,
List, through it all, for the overword:
    Love has wings!

            Alice Williams Brotherton.

—

A THOUSAND YEARS AGO.

THOU and I in spirit-land,
  A thousand years ago,
Watched the waves beat on the strand,
  Ceaseless ebb and flow;
Vowed to love and ever love—
  A thousand years ago.

Thou and I in greenwood shade
  Nine hundred years ago,
Heard the wild dove in the glade
  Murmuring soft and low;
Vowed to love forevermore,—
  Nine hundred years ago.

Thou and I in yonder star,
  Eight hundred years ago,
Saw strange forms of light afar
  In wild beauty glow;
All things change, but love **endures**
  Now as long ago!

Thou and I, in Norman halls,
  Seven hundred years ago,
Heard the warder on the walls
  Loud his trumpet blow,—
Ton amour sera toujours,
  Seven hundred years ago.

Thou and **I** in Germany,
  Six hundred years ago—
Then I bound the red cross on:
  " True love, I must go,—
But we part to meet again
  In the endless flow ! "

Thou and I in Syrian plains,
  Five hundred years ago,
Felt the wild fire in our **veins**
  To a fever flow !
All things die but love lives on
  Now as long ago !

Thou and I in shadow-land,
  Four hundred years ago,
Saw strange flowers bloom on the strand,
  Heard strange breezes blow :
In the ideal love is real,
  This alone **I** know.

Thou and I in Italy,
  Three hundred years ago,
Lived in faith and died for God,
  Felt the fagots glow :
Ever new and ever true,
  Three hundred years ago.

Thou and **I** on Southern seas,
  Two hundred years ago,
Felt the perfumed even-breeze,
Spoke in Spanish by the trees,
  Had no care or woe :
Life went dreamily in song
  Two hundred years ago.

Thou and I 'mid Northern **snows,**
   One hundred years ago,
Led an iron, silent life,
   And **were** glad to flow
Onwards into changing death,
   One hundred years ago.

Thou and I but yesterday
   Met in Fashion's show,
Love, did you remember me,
   Love of long ago?
Yes, we keep the fond oath sworn
   A thousand years ago!

                  Charles Godfrey Leland.

THE ELIXIR.

"**O**H brew me a potion strong and good!
   One golden drop in his wine
Shall charm his sense and fire his blood,
   And bend his will to mine."

Poor child of passion! ask of me
   Elixir of death or sleep,
Or Lethe's stream; but love is free,
   And women must wait and weep.

                  Emma Lazarus.

THE SUNSHINE OF THINE EYES.

THE sunshine of thine eyes,
  O still, celestial beam !
Whatever it touches it fills
  With the light of its lambent gleam.

The sunshine of thine eyes,
  O let it fall on me !
Though I be but a mote in the air,
  I could turn to gold for thee.

George Parsons Lathrop.

UNLOVED.

PALER than the waters white,
  Stood the maiden in the shade,
And more silent than the night
  Were her lips together laid.

Eyes she hid so long and still
  By lids wet with unshed tears,
Hands she loosely clasped at will,
  Though her heart was full of fears.

Never, never, nevermore,
  May her soul with joy be moved,
Silent, silent, silent,—for
  He was silent whom she loved.

Rose Hawthorne Lathrop.

LET SILENCE FALL.

L ET silence fall across the past,
　　Its fitful moods of storm and rain,
　Its weary hours of jealous pain,
Let never heart or speech recall.
　　If memory needs must break the spell,
　　Remember—that I loved you well,
And o'er the rest let silence fall.

Let silence fall between our lives,
　　The one sunlit, with youthful dreams,
　Flushed with the future's hopeful gleams
And held in proud ambition's thrall ;
　　The other worn with anxious tears,
　　And tired grown with gathering years,
Between them now—let silence fall.

And let us part as those who love,
　　Are parted by the hand of Death.
　And one stands hushed, with reverent breath,
Gazing on funeral bier and pall ;
　　But ere we close the coffin lid,
　　Let bitter memories all be hid,
And o'er the grave let silence fall.

James Clarence **Harvey.**

UNCALENDARED.

ONLY a year have thou and I **been friends,**
  If time be counted on our calendar ;
Away with that ! what it begins, it ends ;
  From all eternity, close souls we were,
And shall be, so God grant forevermore,
For two were never faster bound before.

"With God, one day is as a thousand years ;"
  Oh, Love is mighty, God's most blessed name
The more that man his Maker's image bears,
  The more must months and æons be the same.
Love knows not **time,—it is** eternity,
And not a year, that I count **out** with thee !

Charlotte Fiske Bates.

TWO.

HE loved two women; one whose soul **was**
  clean
  As any lily growing on its stalk ;
And one with glowing eyes and sensuous mien,
  Who fired him with her beauty and her talk.

The pure one loved him to the day he died,
　But when he died his dearest friend she wed.
The wanton from the wild world drew aside,
　And no man saw her face till she was dead.

James Berry Bensel.

THE HEART'S CALL.

HE rides away at early light,
　Amid the tingling frost,
And in the mist that sweeps her sight
　His form is quickly lost.

He crosses now the silent stream,
　Now skirts the forest drear,
Whose thickets cast a silver gleam
　From leafage thin and sear.

Long falls the shadow at his back,
　(The morning springs before);
His thoughts fly down the shadowed track,
　And haunt his cottage-door.

Miles gone, upon a hill-top bare
　He draws a sudden rein:
His name, her voice, rings on the air
　When all is still again !

She sits at home, she speaks no word,
  But deeply calls her heart;
And this it is that he has heard,
  Though they are miles apart.

Edith M. Thomas.

IF IT WERE.

LOVE, that thou lov'st me not, too **well I**
    know;
  Yet shouldst thou look to-night on my dead
      face
  For the last time on earth, and there shouldst
      trace
The silent meaning of a heavy woe,
Wouldst thou not feel a pang that it were so?
  Would not regret within thy heart find place,
  That thou didst stay the guerdon and **the**
      grace
Thy lover so besought thee to bestow?
Wouldst thou not feel a want unknown before?
  A something gone familiar grown so long?
A vanished light—a ship gone from the shore—
  A presence passed from out the world's great
      throng?
O love, wouldst thou not miss the voice of
      yore?
  The song-bird flown, wouldst thou not miss
      the song?

James Benjamin Kenyon.

20

COME, look at the woman who died last
    night!
Nay, do not shrink, there's no cause for affright.
Yonder she sits on that low velvet chair—
The one with the jessamine sprays in her hair.

"A fair-looking corpse," did you say, my
    friend?
Just notice her now. What a gracious bend
Of the stately head to some passer-by—
What life in the glance of her velvet eye!

Mark how her bosom beneath its soft lace
Rises and falls—you can see no trace
Of the icy finger that bars the breath,
Of the touch of that monster we know as Death.

And yet in spite of that brilliant smile,
Of each coquettish and playful wile,
In spite of her bloom and her eye's quick light,
She, she is the woman who died last night!

She died out there on the yellow sands;
I saw the despair of her clenchèd hands,
The fading light of her death-struck eye,
The gasp, and the groans of her agony.

For there by a dark rock, crouching low,
This watching woman received her death-blow,
When her lover passed by with his ardent vow
Of love to another ! There they are now !

That captain yonder—the lady 's in blue—
Dancing the lanciers ! In life it is true
That the world wags on no matter who dies—
Victory's drums drown the stricken one's cries.

But I tell you, friend, ere this dreamy morn,
When that woman died a devil was born,
And yonder it sits in that velvet chair,
To weave for the souls of mankind a snare
Out of her rage and her black despair !

Ellie Lee Harden Brook.

WHEN I AM DEAD.

WHEN I am dead what man will say :
    " She used to smile in such a way ;
Her eyes were dark and strangely bright
As are the solemn stars of night "?
What man will say : " Her voice's tone
Was like the far-off winds that moan
Through forest trees? O voice and eyes,
That brought me dreams of paradise ! "

I think no man, when I am dead,
Will say these things that thou hast said
Unto my living face.
And all the bloom and all the grace
Will then be buried out of sight,
Thought of no more, forgotten quite,
As are the flowers of other days,
And songs of birds who sang their praise,
As are the flowers of other springs,
Upon whose grave the wild bird sings.

O flowers and songs of other days!
What sweet new voice will sing your praise?
What choir will celebrate the spring
When love and I went wandering
Between the glades, beneath the trees,
Or by the calm, blue summer seas,
And thought no thing beneath the skies
So lovely as each other's eyes?

When we are dead, when both are gone,
Buried in separate graves alone,
Perchance the restless salt sea wave
Will sing its dirge above my grave;
While you, on some far foreign shore,
May hear the distant ocean roar,
And long at last your arms to twine
About this cold, dead form of mine.

When we are dead, when both are cold,
When love is as a tale that 's told,
Will not our lips, so still and mute,
Still long for love's untasted fruit?
Though lands and seas hold us apart,
Will not my dead heart reach thy heart,
And call to thee from farthest space,
Until we both stand face to face?

Ella Dietz Clymer.

TRIOLET.

HER lips were so near
   That—what else could I do?
You 'll be angry, I fear,
But her lips were so near—
Well, I can't make it clear,
   Or explain it to you,
But—her lips were so near,
   That—what else could I do?

Walter Learned.

SONG FROM "THE CUP OF DEATH."

'T IS better to guess than to see,
   'T is better to dream than to be.
The best of life's loving
Is lost in the proving,
'T is better to dream than to be.

The joy of love's sweetness
Is lost with completeness,
'T is better to dream than to be.

S. Weir Mitchell.

IF I HAD KNOWN.

SHE lay with lilies on her pulseless breast,
   Dim, woodland lilies wet with silver dew.
"Dear heart," he said, "in life she loved them
     best !
  For her sweet sake the fragrant buds were
     blown,
For her in April-haunted nooks they grew—
  . . . Oh, love, if I had known !

"If I had known, when yesterday we walked,
   Her hand in mine, along the hedges fair,
That even then the while we careless talked,
  The shadow of a coming loss was there,
And death's cold hand was leading us apart—
   If I had known the bud she would not wear
Nor touch, lest she should mar that perfect
     grace,
  To-day would press its dewy, golden heart
Against her poor, dead face !

"Last year, when April woods were all aglow,
   She said, 'if it be death to fall asleep,'

And, bending, kissed the lilies sweet **and wet,**
  'A dreamless sleep from which **none** wake
      to weep !—
When I lie down to that long slumber, dear,
  And life for you has dark and empty grown,
Come to me then, and though I shall not hear,
  Lay your sad lips to mine, and whisper **low :**
If I had known ! Oh, love, if I had known !
  That you would not forget.' "

Adelaide D. Rollston.

—

SYLVIA AND THE CHESTNUT FLOWER.

PROUD young head so lightly lifted,
    Crowned with waves of gleaming hair,
Eyes that flash with tell-tale mischief,—
    Fearless eyes to do and dare ;
Cheeks that start **to** sudden flame,
Wilful mouth that none can tame.

Nodding plumes of cream-white blossom,
    Crisp-cut leaves from greener shade,
Laid against the beating bosom,
    'Mid the rippling tresses laid,
Lo, in beauty's fullest **dower,**
Sylvia wears the chestnut flower !

Dark against you forest margin
    Richard found a chestnut tall,

Clambered through the leafy branches,
  Broke the top and crown of all ;
This he brought, and, bolder now,
Gave to her the blossomed bough.

So she took and shyly wears it,—
  Sweet and stately where she stands ;
Subtle perfume floating round her,
  Drooping tassels in her hands ;
Like a Dryad, fair and free
Wandering from her chestnut-tree.

Nay, the human passion enters,—
  Fateful that for good or ill !
For its beauty half she wears it,
  Half for reasons sweeter still ;
Flushed with girlhood's conscious power,
Sylvia wears the chestnut flower !

Summer goes with startled footsteps,
  Autumn strews the yellowing leaves,
Lengths of bloom lie black and shrivelled,
  Where the parting robin grieves ;
Gone the maiden's careless glee,—
Buried 'neath the chestnut tree.

Drooping head and cheek grown paler,
  Wistful mouth and heavy eyes,
Still repeat the same old story,—

How the light of Summer dies;
Both are vanished, gift and giver,—
Once a year and **once forever.**

Years have passed with bloom and beauty,—
    Bloom and love are torn apart;
Still a woman, sad and lonely,
    Keeps one summer **in** her heart,
When, in boyhood's reckless glee,
Richard climbed the chestnut tree.

Still through **life's** unresting fever,
    Dark with passion, wrung with woe,
Dreams a man, in stiller moments,
    Of one summer, long ago,
When, in girlhood's freshest hour,
Sylvia wore the chestnut flower.

Elaine Goodale.

THE FALCON AND THE LILY.

MY darling rides across the sand;
    The wind **is** warm, the wind is bland;
It lifts the pony's glossy mane,
So light and proud she holds his rein.
Not easier bears a leaf the dew
Than she her scarf and kirtle blue,
And on her wrist in bells and jess
The falcon perched for idleness.

That merry bird, O would I were !
In joy with her, in joy with her !

My darling comes not from the bower,
The lowered pennon sweeps the tower ;
The larches droop their tassels low,
And bells are marshalled to and fro.
My heart, my heart beholds her now,
The pallid hands, the saintly brow,
The lily with chill death oppressed
Against the summer of her breast :
That lily pale, O would I were !
In peace with her, in peace with her !

Louise Imogen Guiney.

SONG FROM "IDUN."

DROOP and darken, eyes of blue,
    Love hath only tears for you,
Love, begone, and lightly flee.
Since thy smiles are not for me

Lips of scarlet, quench your fire,
Torches vain of love's desire,
    Love, begone, and lightly flee,
    Since thy sweets are not for me.

Sink, ye swelling breasts of snow,
Baby fingers ne'er to know,
Love, begone, and lightly flee,
Since thy fruits are not for me.

Harry Lyman Koopman.

"FOR BETTER FOR WORSE."

QUOTH he: "Sweetheart, thou art young
    and fair,
And thy story has just begun;
    But I am as old
    As a tale that 's told,
And the days of my youth are done."
"O'er ruins olden the clinging moss
Doth a mantle of velvet spread:
    Shall the climbing flower
    Be more to the tower
Than I to my Love?" she said.

Quoth he: "Sweetheart, thou hast lands and
    gold,
And thou knowest not want nor woe;
    As a beggar poor
    I stand at thy door
And I only can love thee so."
"Through leafless forests the sunbeams creep,
All the wealth of their gold to shed;

And are they more fair
To the woodland bare
Than I to my Love?" she said.

Quoth he: "Sweetheart, thou art good and kind
And wouldst never the lowest spurn;
But the storm of life
With its toil and strife
Has rendered me harsh and stern."
" The brooklet murmurs its sweetest lays
As it makes for the rocks ahead:
Shall the streamlet's song
Be more brave and strong
Than I for my Love?" she said.

Quoth he: "Sweetheart, thou art blithe and gay,
And thou never hast known a care;
But my face is worn
And my heart is torn
With the sorrow I 've had to bear."
" The stars ne'er spangle the sapphire sky
Till the brightness of day has fled:
Shall the pale starlight
Be truer to night
Than I to my Love?" she said.

Quoth he: " Sweetheart, who art young and fair,
Will thy wonderful love to me
Through sorrow or shame
Be always the same?"

"Nay, it rather will grow," said she.
Again he cried : "Will it last, Sweetheart,
   Till thy lover lies cold and dead,
      And thy latest breath
      Has been hushed in death?"
" Aye, longer than that," she said.

Ellen Thorneycroft-Fowler.

HOW STRANGE IT WILL BE!

How strange it will be, love—how strange,
      when we two
   Shall be what all lovers become :
You frigid and faithless, I cold and untrue—
You thoughtless of me, and I careless of you—
Our pet names grown rusty with nothing to
      do—
Love's bright web unravelled, and rent, and
      worn through,
   And life's loom left empty—ah, hum !
      Ah, me,
         How strange it will be !

How strange it will be when the witchery goes,
   Which makes me seem lovely to-day ;
When your thought of me loses its *couleur de
      rose ;*
When every day serves some new thought to
      disclose ;

When you find I 've cold eyes, and an every-
   day nose,
And wonder you could for a moment suppose
  I was out of the commonplace way—
    Ah, **me**,
      How strange it will be !

How strange it will be, love—how strange, when
   we meet
  With just **a** chill touch of the hand !
When my pulses no longer delightedly beat
At the thought of your coming, the sound of
   your feet—
When I watch not your going, far down **the**
   long street ;
When your dear, loving voice, now so thrill-
   ingly sweet,
  Grows harsh in reproach or command—
    Ah, me,
      How strange it will be !

How strange it will be, when we willingly stay
  Divided the weary day through !
Or, getting remotely apart as we may,
Sit chilly and silent, with nothing to say,
Or coolly converse **on** the news of the **day**,
In a wearisome, old married-folks **sort of way** !
  I shrink from the picture—don't you ?
    Ah, me,
      How strange it will be !

Dear love, if our hearts *do* grow torpid and old,
  As many others have done ;
If we let our love perish with hunger and cold,
If we dim all life's diamonds, and tarnish its
      gold,
If we choose to live wretched, and die uncon-
      soled,
 T will be strangest of all things that ever were
      told
    As happening under the sun !
      Ah, me,
          How strange it *will* be !

Frank E. Holliday.

UNIDENTIFIED.

MY KING.

YOU are all that I have to live for,
  All that I want to love,
All that the whole world holds for me,
  Of faith in a world above.
You came—and it seemed too mighty
  For my human heart to hold,
It seemed in its sacred glory
  Like a glimpse through the gates of gold,
Like a life in the primal Eden,
  Created and formed anew—
This charm of a perfect manhood
  That I realize in you.

God created me a woman
  With a nature just as true
As the blue eternal ocean,
  As the heavens over you.
And you are mine till your Maker calls you,
  Your soul and your body, Sweet!

Your breath and the whole of your being,
　From your kingly head to your feet ;
Your eyes and the light that is in them,
　Your lips with their maddening wine,
Your arms with their passionate clasp, my king,
　Your body and soul are mine !

No power whatsoever,
　No will but God's alone,
Can take you from my keeping,
　You are His and mine alone.

I know not when, if ever,
　I know not where, or how,
Death's hand may try the fetters
　That bind me here and now ;
But some day, when God beckons,
　Where rise His fronded palms,
My soul shall cross the river,
　And lay you in His arms ;—
Forever and forever
　Beyond the silent sea,
You will rest in the Arms Eternal,
　And still belong to me !

YOU kissed **me** ! My head had dropped low on
    your breast,
With **a** feeling of shelter and infinite rest ;
And a holy emotion my tongue dared not speak
Flashed up in a flame from my heart to my
    cheek.
Your arms held me fast. O, your arms were so
    bold !
Heart beat against heart in their passionate
    fold ;
Your glances seemed drawing **my** soul through
    my eyes
As the sun draws the mist from the seas to the
    skies ;
And **your** lips clung to mine till I prayed in
    my bliss,
They might never unclasp from that rapturous
    kiss.

You kissed me ! My heart and my breath and
    my will,
In delicious joy for the moment stood still.
Life had for me then no temptations, no charms,
No vista of pleasure outside of your arms ;
And were I this instant an angel, possessed
Of the peace and the joy that are given the blest,

I would fling my white robes unrepiningly down
And tear from my forehead its beautiful crown
To nestle once more in that haven of rest,
Your lips upon mine, my head on your breast.

You kissed me ! My soul in a bliss so divine
Reeled and swooned like a drunken man foolish
    with wine ;
And I thought 't were delicious to die then, if
    death
Could but come while my lips were yet moist
    with your breath ;
'T were delicious to die if my heart might grow
    cold
While your arms clasped me round in that pas-
    sionate fold !
And these are the questions I ask day and night :
Must my life taste but once such exquisite de-
    light ?
Would you care if your breast were my shelter
    as then ?
And if you were here would you kiss me again ?

SCORNED.

SCORNED by a man that is weaker than I !
    Down at my feet in the dust he shall lie,
Down at my feet in the dust he shall pray
For the love that he values so lightly to-day.

He shall turn from the maiden so rosy and fair,
He shall tire of the pale golden hue of her hair,
He shall turn from the eyes that are sunny and
    blue
To the heart that he deems so forgiving and
    true.

And then he shall learn when he asks for a
    bride
That a true woman's love is outweighed by her
    pride,
And when pale with anguish he kneels at my
    feet,
He shall read in my eyes that revenge is most
    sweet.

I will teach him to play with a rattlesnake's
    tongue,
I will teach him the tiger to rob of its young,
I will teach him 't were better a man were
    unborn
If the love of a proud-hearted woman he scorn.

DO YOU.

Do you feel sometimes in your dreaming
    The weight of my head on your breast?
Or the velvety touch of my kisses
    On your lips in passion impressed?

Do you hold me sometimes in your dreaming
  In a rapturous clasp on your heart?
Or cry in the depth of your yearning
  "'T is cruel to keep us apart?"

Does my hand with its lingering caresses
  Touch yours with its magic again,
Till starting you wake from the pressure
  To find that your dreaming was vain?

Though light as the fall of a rose leaf,
  You 'd feel the sweet weight of my kiss
And starting you 'd waken to kiss me,
  And taste love's ineffable bliss?

Ah! never again shall I see you,
  Nor look in your proud, grand face,
Ne'er feel the sweet balm of your kisses,
  Or thrill to your tender embrace.

For our lives lie asunder forever,
  More wide than the cruel sea,
But I love you! I love you! **I love you!**
  And in dreams I will linger with thee.

JACK AND I.

I WAS so tired of Jack, poor boy,
  And Jack was tired of me ;
Most longed for sweets will soonest cloy ;
  Fate had been kind, and we,
Two foolish spendthrift hearts, made waste
Of life's best gifts with eager haste.

Oh ! tired we were.   Time seems so long
  When every thing goes well !
The walls of home rose grim and strong ;
  Like prisoners in a cell
We clanked our marriage chains, and pined
For freedom we had left behind.

Tired, tired of love and peace were we,
  Of every day's calm bliss !
We had no goal to win, since he
  Was mine and I was his ;
And so we sighed in mute despair,
And wished each other anywhere.

But sorrow came one day—the pain
  Of death's dark, awful fear ;
Oh, then our hearts beat warm again ;
  Then each to each was dear.
It seemed that life could nothing lack,
While Jack had me and I had Jack !

PLATONIC.

I KNEW it the first of the summer—
   I knew it the same at the end—
That you and your love were plighted,
   But could n't you be my friend?
Could n't we sit in the twilight,
   Could n't we talk on the **shore,**
With only a pleasant friendship
   To bind us, and nothing more?

There was never a **word of** nonsense
   Spoken between us two,
Though we lingered oft in the garden
   Till the roses were wet with dew.
We touched on a thousand subjects—
   The moon, and the stars above,
But our talks were tinctured with science,
   With never a hint of love.

" **A** wholly platonic friendship,"
   You said I had proved to you,
" Could bind a man and a woman
   The whole long season through,
With never **a** hint of folly,
   Though both are in their youth."
What would you have said, my lady,
   If you had known the truth?

Had I done what my mad heart prompted—
  Gone down on my knees to you,
And told you my passionate story,
  There in the dusk **and dew ;**
My burning, burdensome story,
  Hidden and hushed **so long ;**
My story of hopeless loving—
  Say, would you have thought it wrong ?

But I fought **with** my heart, and conquered—
  I hid my wound **from** sight ;
You were going away in the morning,
  And I said a calm good-night.
But now, when I sit in the twilight,
  Or when I walk **by the** sea,
That friendship, quite " platonic,"
  Comes surging **over me.**
And a passionate longing fills me,
  For the roses, the dusk, and the dew—
For the beautiful summer vanished—
  For the moonlit talks—and you.

HER LAST WORDS.

NO ! let me alone—'t is better so,
  My way and yours are widely far apart.
Why **should you** stop to grieve about my woe ?
  And **why should** I not step across your heart ?
A man's heart **is a** poor thing at the best,
And yours is no whit better than the rest.

I loved you once! Ah, yes! Perhaps, **I did.**
  Women are curious things, you know, and
    strange,
And hard to understand, and then besides,
  The key of her soul's music oft doth change,
And so—ah! do not look at me that way!
I loved you once, but that was yesterday!

Sometimes **a** careless word **doth rankle** deep—
  So deep that it can change a heart like this,
And blot out all the long sweet throbbing hours
  That went before, crowned gold with rap-
    turous bliss ;
So deep that it can blot out hours divine,
And make a heart as hard and cold as mine.

Nay, do not speak.   I never can forget ;
  So let us say good-by, and go our ways.
Mayhap the pansies will start from the dust
  Of our past days—the slumbrous, happy days
When I was trusting, and life knew no grief,
But blossomed with my clinging, sweet belief.

Good-by! Good-by! Part of my **life** you take.
  Its fairest part.   Nay, do not touch my lips.
Once they were yours, but now, oh, my lost love!
  I would not have you touch my finger tips,
And saying this I feel no chill of pain,
I cannot even weep above my slain.

If God cares aught for women who have loved
  And worshipped idols false, I trust he will
Keep us so far apart that never more
  Our paths may cross.   Why are you standing
      still ?
Good-by, I say. This is the day's dim close ;
Our love is no more worth than last year's rose.

LONGINGS.

IF I could hold your hands to-night,
  Just for a little while, and know
That only I, of all the world,
  Possessed them so.

A slender shape in that old chair,
  If I could see you here to-night,
Between me and the twilight pale—
  So light and frail.

Your cool white dress, its folding lost
  In one broad sweep of shadow gray ;
Your weary head just drooped aside,
  That sweet old way.

Bowed like a flower-cup dashed with rain,
  The darkness crossing half your face,
And just the glimmer of a smile
  For one to trace.

If I could see your eyes that reach
    Far out into the farthest sky,
Where past the trail of dying suns,
    The old years lie.

Or touch your silent lips to-night,
    And steal the sadness from their smile,
And find the last kiss they have kept
    This weary while!

If it could be—Oh, all in vain
    The restless trouble of my soul
Sets, as the great tides of the moon,
    Toward your control!

In vain the longings of the lips,
    The eye's desire, and the pain ;
The hunger of the heart—O love,
    Is it in vain?

LAST NIGHT.

LAST night, within the little curtained room,
    Where the gay music sounded faintly clear,
And silver lights came stealing through the
        gloom,
    You told the tale that women love to hear ;
You told it well, with firm hands clasping mine,
    And deep eyes glowing with a tender light.
Mere acting? But your prayer was half divine
                Last night, last night.

Ah, you had much to offer ; wealth enough
  To gild the future, and a path of ease
For one whose way is somewhat dark and
      rough ;
  New friends—life calm as summer seas
And something (was it love ?) to keep us true
  And make us precious in each other's sight.
Ah, then, indeed, my heart's resolve I knew,
          Last night, last night.

Let the world go, with all its dross and pelf !
  Only for one, like Portia, could I say :
" I would be trebled twenty times myself " ;
  Only for one, and he is far away ;
His voice came back to me, distinct and dear,
  And thrilled me with the pain of lost delight ;
The present faded, but the past was clear,
          Last night, last night.

If others answéred as I answered then,
  We would hear less, perchance, of blighted
      lives ;
There would be truer women, nobler men,
  And fewer dreary homes and faithless wives ;
Because I could not give you all my best,
  I gave you nothing. Judge me—was I right?
You may thank heaven that I stood the test
          Last night, last night.

LIFE.

WE meet and part ; the world is wide ;
　　We journey onward side by side
A little way, and then again
Our paths diverge ; a little pain,
A silent yearning of the heart
For what had grown of life a part,
A feeling of somewhat bereft,
A closer clasp on what is left,
A shadow passing o'er the sun,
Then gone, and light again has come.
We meet and part, and then forget,
And life holds blessings for us yet.

WHO SHALL GO FIRST?

WHO shall go first to the shadowy land
　　My love or I ?
Whose will it be in grief to stand
And press the cold, unanswering hand,
Wipe from the brow the dew of death,
And catch the softly fluttering breath,
Breathe the loved name nor hear reply,
In anguish watch the glazing eye—
　　His or mine?

Which shall bend over the wounded sod,
　　　My love or I?
Commending the precious soul to God,
Till the doleful fall of the muffled clod
Startles the mind to a consciousness
Of its bitter anguish and life-distress,
Dropping the pall o'er the love-lit past
With a mournful murmur, " The last, the last "—
　　　My love or I?

Which shall return to the desolate home,
　　　My love or I?
And list for a step that shall never come,
And hark for a voice that must still be dumb,
While the half-stunned senses wander back
To the cheerless life and thorny track,
Where the silent room and the vacant chair
Have memories sweet and hard to bear—
　　　My love or I?

Ah, then, perchance, to that mourner there,
　　　My love or I!
Wrestling with anguish and deep despair,
An angel shall come through the gates of
　　prayer,
And the burning eyes shall cease to weep,
And the sobs melt down in a sea of sleep,
While fancy, freed from the chains of day,
Through the shadowy dreamland floats away—
　　　My love or I?

22

And then, methinks, **on** that boundary land,
My love and I !
The mourned and the mourner together shall
stand,
Or walk by those rivers of shining sand,
Till the dreamer awakened at dawn of day,
Finds the stone of his sepulchre rolled away,
And over the cold, dull waste of death,
The warm, bright sunlight of holy faith,
My love and I ?

OH, JESSIE, WHAR' YO' GON'?

OH, Jessie, laughin' Jessie, whar' yo' gon'?
Is yo' wand'rin' in de medder,
Whar' we used to roam togedder?
Is yo' wand'rin' t'rough de cotton or de co'n?
Oh, Jessie, doan' yo' hear me?
Is yo' laughin' sperrit near me,
Or has you learn' to fear me
An' to sco'n?

Dey done tole me, Jessie, honey, yo' is dead—
Dat yo' sperrit is a libin'
Wid de angels up in heaben,
An' yo' nebber comin' back to me, dey said ;
But I saw yo' eyes abeamin',
An' I 's sho' I was n't dreamin',
For de moonlight was a gleamin'
Oberhead.

Den I tried to catch yo' eye an' feel yo' han',
   But de minnit I come near yo',
   Fur to fondle and to cheer yo',
Yo' done glide away an' leab me whar' I stan',
   Yo' done leab me dar a cryin',
   An' my heart widin me dyin',
   While de night wind crep' a sighin'
      T'rough de lan'.

Oh, my angel! Oh, my Jessie! Am it true?
   Is yo' gone from me for eber
   Across de sperrit riber?
Den I soon will come across dat riber, too.
   For my eyes wid tears am achin',
   An' my heart wid grief am breakin'
   An' my cabin am forsaken,
      Widout you.

IMPERISHABLE REMEMBRANCE.

THEY say, if our beloved dead
   Should seek the old, familiar place,
Some stranger would be there instead,
   And they would find no welcoming face.

I cannot tell how it might be
   In other homes; but this I know:
Could my lost darling come to me,
   That she would never find it so.

Ofttimes the flowers have come and gone,
  Ofttimes the winter winds have blown,
The while her peaceful rest went on,
  And I have learned to live alone.

Have slowly learned from day to day
  In all life's task to bear my part;
But whether grave, or whether gay,
  I hide her memory in my heart.

Fond, faithful love has blest my way,
  And friends are round me true and tried,
They have their places—hers to-day
  Is empty as the day she died.

How would I spring with bated breath,
  And joy too deep for word or sign,
To take my darling home from death,
  And once again to call her mine!

I dare not dream the blissful dream,
  It fills my heart with wild unrest;
Where yonder cold white marbles gleam,
  She still must slumber—God knows best!

But this I know, that those who say
  Our best beloved would find no place,
Have never hungered every day—
  Though years and years for one dear face!

"THY DEAR HANDS WILL SWIFTLY DRAW ME IN."

O NCE, in the twilight of a wintry day,
    One passed me silent, struggling on his way,
With head bowed low and hands that burdens bore,
And saw not how, a little space before,

A woman watched his coming, where the light
Poured a glad welcome through a window bright,
Set thick with flowers that showed no fairer bloom
Than her sweet face, turned outward to the gloom

Yet when his foot, with quick, impatient stride,
But touched the step, the door swung open wide ;
Soft hands reached swiftly out, with eager hold,
And drew the dear one in from storm and cold.

O love ! whose eyes, from some celestial height,
Behold me toiling, burdened through the night,
Tender of every blast at which I cower,
Yet smiling still, to know how brief the hour ;

Keeping within thy radiant, love-lit home,
Some glad surprise to whisper when I come—
'T is but a breath till I the door shall win
And thy dear hands will softly draw me in.

THE END.

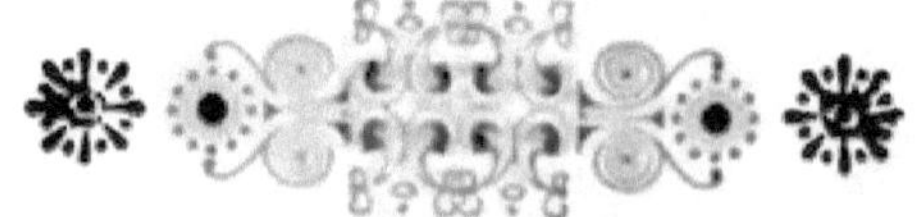

INDEX OF SUBJECTS.

Vol II—23

THE END.

Ariel Booklets

1. **The Gold Bug.** By Edgar Allan Poe.
2. **Rab and his Friends and Marjorie Fleming.** By John Brown, M.D.
3. **The Culprit Fay.** By Joseph Rodman Drake.
4. **Our Best Society.** By George William Curtis.
5. **Sonnets from the Portuguese.** By Elizabeth Barrett Browning
6. **The School for Scandal.** By Richard Brinsley Sheridan.
7. **The Rivals.** By Richard Brinsley Sheridan.
8. **The Good-Natured Man.** By Oliver Goldsmith.
9. **Sweetness and Light.** By Matthew Arnold.
10. **Lyrics.** By Robert Browning.
11. **L'Allegro and Il Penseroso.** By John Milton.
12. **Thanatopsis, Flood of Years,** etc. By William Cullen Bryant.

The Ariel Shakespeare

Forty volumes. Each play in a separate volume
Five hundred outline illustrations
Each play annotated

**Bound in full flexible red morocco,
in a box, each, 65 cents**

LIST OF VOLUMES

COMEDIES:

Tempest
Two Gentlemen of Verona
Merry Wives of Windsor
Measure for Measure
Comedy of Errors
Much Ado About Nothing
Love's Labour 's Lost
Midsummer Night's Dream
Merchant of Venice
As You Like It
Taming of the Shrew
All 's Well that Ends Well
Twelfth Night
Winter's Tale

TRAGEDIES:

Troilus and Cressida
Coriolanus
Titus Andronicus
Romeo and Juliet
Timon of Athens
Julius Cæsar
Macbeth
Hamlet
King Lear
Othello
Antony and Cleopatra
Cymbeline

HISTORIES:

King John
Richard II.
Henry IV. *First Part*
Henry IV. *Second Part*
Henry V.

Henry VI. *First Part*
Henry VI. *Second Part*
Henry VI. *Third Part*
Richard III.
Henry VIII.

Pericles
Sonnets

Poems
Glossary

THE ARIEL IRVING

12 volumes, size 5½ by 3½ inches, printed from good clear type, on paper of excellent quality, bound in full flexible red morocco . . per set, $9.00

COMPRISES—

The Sketch Book, in two volumes, containing many of the author's masterpieces, including "Rip Van Winkle" and "The Legend of Sleepy Hollow."

The Alhambra, in two volumes.

"The beautiful Spanish 'Sketch Book,' and the 'Alhambra.'"—W. H. PRESCOTT.

The Tales of a Traveller, in two volumes.

"The variety of these tales makes this one of the most delightful of all of Irving's works."—Hartford Courant.

Bracebridge Hall, or The Humorists, in two volumes.

"The great charm and peculiarity of this work consists now, as on former occasions, in the singular sweetness of the composition."—LORD JEFFREY, in Edinburgh Review.

Knickerbocker's History of New York, from the beginning of the World to the end of the Dutch Dynasty, by Diedrich Knickerbocker. Two volumes.

"The most excellently jocose 'History of New York.' Our sides have been absolutely sore with laughing." — Sir WALTER SCOTT

"A book of unwearying pleasantry."
— EDWARD EVERETT.

Wolfert's Roost, and other papers, in one volume.

"The papers in the present volume are among his latest and most charming productions."—Chicago Tribune.

Crayon Miscellany, containing the ever delightful "Tour of the Prairies" and "Abbotsford." One volume.

G. P. PUTNAM'S SONS, New York and London

www.ingramcontent.com/pod-product-compliance
Lightning Source LLC
Chambersburg PA
CBHW021527110726
47902CB00004B/784